Reasonable Doubts
by
Kyra Lennon

To
Vicky
Lovely to meet you!

Love Kyra Lennon
x

1

Acknowledgements

It takes a team of people to put a book together, and for my last few books, I have relied on very few people. This time, I decided to go back to the start – so to speak – and gather a team of beta readers to help me iron out any issues.

It was the best decision I ever made.

I want to send a huge thank you to Clare, Sarah, Keren, Karen, Caroline and Krissy for your hard work and kind comments. You guys are invaluable!

Chapter 1
Darcy

"Are you sure about this?"

I stared at my best friend through the glass, watching as his fists clenched, eager to reach out to me. Except he couldn't. No contact visits were all Matteo Torres was allowed now. My heart squeezed in my chest because I'd have given just about anything to hug him tight. To promise him, not just with words but with actions, that I wouldn't let him down.

"I'm sure," I said firmly. "I didn't do this much research to let you down at the last hurdle."

He shook his head, his overgrown dark curls whipping around his face. "This isn't the last hurdle and you know it. This is dangerous, Darcy."

"What else am I supposed to do?" I hissed, lowering my voice and leaning forward so there was less chance of being overheard. "Let you stay here and rot? Let those asshole cops get away with what they did to you? We've exhausted every other option."

"I know, but I don't want this to end with both of us stuck behind bars for the rest of our lives. Or worse. Maybe we should just leave it with the lawyers."

Another painful twist in my heart. Thirty-seven days ago, Matteo had been found guilty of murdering his wife, and since then, the hope in his deep brown eyes had all but burned out. For the ten months he'd awaited trial, optimism blazed, certain reasonable doubt would be proved. We'd both underestimated how unwilling a jury would be to accept that the police could possibly be the bad guys. The word 'guilty' had echoed around the courtroom like a gunshot, ricocheting off the walls and hitting me right in the heart.

Now I sat in front of a shadow of a man, his last shred of faith hanging by a rapidly fraying thread.

"As public defenders go, you've been lucky, Matty. But you know neither of us can put up the kind of money needed to hire a lawyer who can truly make this go away." I shrugged. "It's down to us now. Down to me."

"I don't want you to risk your life for me." His gaze dipped before returning to my face. "I can't ask you to do that."

"You didn't ask. You don't belong in here. If there's a chance that I—"

"Darcy, this is insane! *You* are insane for even considering it."

That much I couldn't deny. He'd tried every step of the way to talk me out of it, but I wouldn't budge. There was nothing he could do or say to change my mind now.

"No. The people who thought they could set you up are insane for thinking we'd let this go."

The smallest hint of a smile flickered, but it died on his lips as he reached up again, his hand moving toward the glass before falling down when he remembered he couldn't touch me. I placed my own hand against the glass; it was the best I could do. On the other side, he did the same.

"I'm getting you out of here, Matteo." I told him. "Whatever it takes."

A few hours later, I sat on the edge of my bed, waiting for my cab to take me to Midnight Rodeo—a country and western-style bar in the city—to begin phase one of my insane plan. But as clichéd as the phrase was, desperate times really did call for desperate measures.

As I stared at the framed photograph in my hands, I tried to steady my nerves and stop the downpour of tears that pricked the backs of my eyes. The people smiling back at me had had no idea where life would take us. No idea that we wouldn't always have the freedom we had back then. God, we were so happy. So naïve. The Matteo in the photo was the real Matteo. His wide grin beamed at me, his dark skin almost glowing with joy as he stood beside his new bride. Rebecca Torres had looked stunning on their wedding day. Her dark hair fell in perfect curls, framing her face. Her own smile was radiant, and her deep brown eyes sparkled. I stood beside her, the only bridesmaid on my best friends' big day. I barely recognized myself. The stress of the last year had taken its toll on me almost as much as it had on Matteo. My chestnut-colored hair had lost its shine, so much so that I'd made an appointment at my salon that afternoon to give it the pick-me-up it needed. And make-up? I barely bothered with that anymore, sticking to the absolute minimum when I went to work. Make-up was another thing I'd had to reacquaint myself with in order to set my plan in motion. If this was going to work out, I needed to look good. Irresistible, in fact. There was a fine line between irresistible and slutty, especially to a guy like Detective Finn Drake, and I needed to stay on the right side of that line. I wore close fitting jeans, black, heeled ankle boots, and a long-sleeved black top that clung to my curves. The lace detail in the sleeves added a touch of class, or at least I hoped so. The neckline was low, but not *too* low.

A ripple of panic shot down my spine as the reality of coming face to face with Finn Drake trickled into my mind.

What the hell are you doing, Darcy? This is crazy dangerous.

But as I looked down at the photo of my friends again, I knew I didn't have any other choice. Justice had not been served. Matteo was in jail, grieving for his wife and his freedom, and I was grieving for my friends who had both lost their lives in very different ways. It wasn't okay. And I was the only person left who had a shot at finding out the truth.

Chapter 2
Darcy

The stench of beer hit me as soon as I walked through the door, and I blinked a few times to stop it from overpowering me. It wasn't my first time at Midnight Rodeo, of course. I'd been there alone on random days of the week when I knew Finn Drake wouldn't be. I'd been there on a couple of occasions with my colleagues from the coffee house when he *was* there, just so, when he saw me, it wouldn't seem as if I'd showed up out of nowhere. I'd sat outside in my car hiding in the shadows more times than I'd been inside, just watching. Learning his routine. Biding my time for when I could finally put my plan into action.

My eyes scanned the room and, just as I expected, he hadn't arrived yet. He never arrived before eight-thirty and it was only eight-fifteen. This gave me time to throw down a glass of wine–maybe two–before he arrived so I could calm my shaking hands.

Blowing out a breath, I held my head high to at least feign confidence, and strode toward the bar, my heeled boots clicking against the wooden floor. Each step perfectly matched the hammering in my heart. In reality, there was enough noise from other patrons and the country music playing through the speakers that nobody would notice me. I chuckled to myself–not for the first time–that Mr. Tough Guy Cop hung out in a country music-playing bar. I'd have thought a badass Chicago cop would have spent his leisure time somewhere significantly cooler. Not that there was anything wrong with the place; it had a definite charm about it. It just felt at odds with the image he portrayed.

As I sat on a stool at the bar and ordered a glass of red wine, I conjured up a picture of Detective Drake in my mind. He was tall and slim with sandy-colored hair, pale blue eyes, and thin, almost mean-looking lips. I'd have guessed he was around thirty, maybe a little older. Physically he was about a foot too tall and built all wrong to fit in with my tastes, but at that point, getting closer to him was my only hope of finding out the truth. And I would get as close to him as it took, for as long as it took to elicit the truth from him.

Too bad he's not one of those dumb cops who'll just spill his guts after a couple of beers. No. Drake was smart, and whatever way I played this, the game wouldn't be over in a day. It could take months, more even. But it would be worth it if I could trip him up. Find out what exactly had gone down the night Rebecca was murdered, and how the murder weapon had ended up in Matteo's garage.

Police corruption. Those words are cried out by a lot of people, and over and over it gets squashed down, labelled as an excuse for those who refuse to face up to what they've done. And sometimes that's true. But not for Matteo. He loved his wife, no matter what she'd done.

I gave the bartender a small smile as he offered me my drink and I handed over the cash. It had been one shock after another. Matteo had found out Rebecca had been cheating on him three weeks before she was murdered. Aside from me, Matteo told no-one. Didn't even tell Rebecca he knew. A ripple of anger toward her surged through me, because how could she do that? I'd wanted to confront her but Matteo made me swear to keep my mouth shut. Personally, I wasn't sure I'd ever love anyone so much that I'd forgive them for cheating, but Matteo really did. That was part of what made the whole thing so tragic. He'd kept quiet in order to keep her, but in the end? He lost her anyway.

The tiny hairs on my arms stood to attention as I heard Detective Drake's voice beside me. It was unmistakable with its deep, gravelly tone. Hot as hell, actually, but the man himself was despicable, so I told my body to calm down. I may have been planning to make a move on him, but it most definitely wasn't because I wanted to.

"This might be a little cliché, sweetheart, but… you looking for some company?"

Without turning my head, I swiveled my eyes in his direction, mostly to check if he was talking to me. When I saw his eyes fixed on me, I said, "I'm not a hooker."

Glancing down at my outfit, I was positive I didn't look like one, but that line he'd used. It was a little too *Pretty Woman* for my liking. *God. I'm worse than a hooker. Willing to screw him for info. I'm not even getting paid.* Even though I was prepared to give it away for free if it got me what I needed, I hoped it wouldn't come down to that. *Prayed* it wouldn't.

He let out a loud, throaty laugh. "Good to know. 'Cos I'm a cop, and if you *were* a hooker, I'd have to arrest you, and that would be a damn shame."

Slowly, I turned my head toward him, my skin prickling at the way his eyes were assessing me. *Shake it off. You have to do this.* Giving him my best Oscar winning performance, I said, "Wow, really? I have so much respect for cops in this city. Cops all over, actually. A commendable profession."

Okay, just to be clear, I wasn't completely lying. I did have a lot of respect for cops who did their jobs correctly. Finn Drake? Not so much.

His thin lips curved into a smile. "Would you like to join me for a drink?"

My gaze flicked up and down his body, taking in the dark green shirt that clung to his lean but muscular chest, and his casual blue jeans. I was always a little taken aback by how different he looked in casual clothes, compared to his smart, perfectly ironed work suits. If I was honest, I'd say he kinda rocked both styles, but still, he wasn't my type. Right?

Focus, Darcy.

With a small shake of my head to bring my attention back to him, I fixed him with a grin. "Sure. But maybe you should tell me your name before this gets awkward."

A glimmer of… something flashed in his eyes before he held his hand out to me. "Finn Drake."

Taking it, I shook it firmly. "Alicia Hadley."

What? You think I'd give him my real name? Hell, no. This wasn't me picking up a hot date, this was me doing a job, and to do that, I had to play a role. Dig into the depths of myself and figure out what would attract this dude and make him want me. I couldn't allow any of the real me to slip through; I had to be… *nice.*

Another smirk played on Finn's lips. "Alicia," he repeated, as if relishing the feel of my name on his tongue. "Let's go take a seat."

As he stepped in front of me to lead the way, I dropped my guard for a few seconds, relieved this part had been so easy. Now? Well, this was where I had to really make it work. My insides were vibrating with nerves, but I took another gulp of wine to ease my panic. *Besides, nothing will happen tonight anyway, right? This is a simple getting to know you exercise.*

For now.

**

Five glasses of wine later, I was sure.

I hated this smug fuck.

Finn Drake was every bit as cocky in the real world as he was in court. When I'd watched him throughout the trial, whether he was on the stand or just watching the proceedings, he'd had this air of over-confidence, but a small part of me had wondered whether it was for show.

Wondered if he was playing the tough guy to intimidate. Nope. He truly did have his head lodged that far up his ass. It was apparent in every word he spoke, telling me about how quickly he'd been promoted and how many criminals he'd helped put behind bars. How he'd won some kind of award for his hard work and dedication. Blah, blah, blah.

Had I not been committed to my mission, I'd have left hours ago. Instead, I continued to smile and listen as if this were the most riveting conversation I'd ever been involved in. As the time ticked away though, a steady trickle of worry dripped into my veins that I hadn't managed to do what I'd wanted to do. That I hadn't made him want to see me again. Hadn't made him want *me*. In my defense, he'd hardly given me a chance to dazzle him since he'd only talked about himself the whole time, but this was my one shot at making my mark on him.

It was time to take things up a notch.

The bar was now full to bursting, with the sound of chatter, music, and clinking glasses making it difficult for me to hear Finn's endless monologue of self-praise. Wasn't too hard to think of a way to move things along.

When Finn paused for breath, I placed my hand on his knee and leaned in closer to him, making absolutely certain he got a decent view of my cleavage as I did so, while maintaining an expression of wide-eyed innocence on my face.

"It's getting kinda loud in here," I said. "Do you want to maybe walk me home? I might even invite you inside for a coffee if you ask nicely."

His gaze flicked briefly down to my chest before looking back up into my eyes. "That's a little forward, Miss Hadley. Didn't your momma ever tell you not to invite strangers back to your apartment?"

I ran my tongue across my lower lip then smiled. "I never

do what my momma tells me." *He doesn't need to know my momma was never around long enough to tell me anything.* I quirked my head to one side. "Besides, you're a cop. Who could I possibly be safer with?"

It took all my strength not to choke on the words.

Finn's throaty chuckle only served to remind me how completely *un*safe this whole situation was, but my comment seemed to have the desired effect on him. "I'll walk you home. Can't have anything bad happening to you, can we?"

With a sweet smile, I said, "Thank you. It's not far."

It really wasn't. My apartment was just four blocks away from the bar, and on the walk back, it occurred to me that it might be a huge mistake to take him there. What if he tried to find out more about me from my address? If I were a cop, I'd use every resource I had to check out potential dates. And Drake wasn't stupid; no one who was smart enough to frame an innocent man would be stupid enough to not find out who they were involved with. *Fuck. I might actually have to screw him tonight and hope it blows his mind enough to give him amnesia.*

If Finn frequented Midnight Rodeo, perhaps he didn't live far away either. I didn't ask, though. Too many questions too soon and I'd blow my cover. This was only day one. If I wanted to see this through, I had to keep playing my part of single-girl-meets-cop.

"So, tell me something about you," Finn said, as we walked through the busy Chicago streets. The bright lights from late night stores and clubs lit our way, and people passed us in a blur as they hurried along to their next destination. Pre-Matteo's arrest, I would have been one of those people heading out to the city's clubs for a kickass night out, but things were different now.

"Me?" I couldn't help wondering why it had taken him so long to ask me a question. *No wonder he's single.* "Not much to tell. I'm just an ordinary girl trying to survive in this crazy world."

From the corner of my eye, I saw him turn his head toward me. "Nah. I don't believe it for a second. Ordinary girls don't hang out in bars alone. I've seen you in there before, you know? But never alone."

"Well… I work in a coffee house. I'm surrounded by people all day long." I met his eye for a second. "Sometimes it's nice to be somewhere and just sit. Not needing to talk to anyone, just observing others. Is that so strange?"

A surprised smile crossed his face. "That's the reason I go there alone, too. Well, that and the possibility of meeting a beautiful woman."

His smirk almost made me roll my eyes until I remembered that it was my mission to keep him interested in me, and if that meant keeping a firm grip on my snark, then so be it.

"So, why me?" I asked, stepping just a fraction closer to him as we walked so our arms lightly brushed. "I wasn't the only woman in the bar tonight."

"You were the only one in there who looked like she has a story to tell. Pretty women in bars… I see them all the time. But you? Different kind of pretty."

Again, I glanced up at him. Not what I'd expected from the guy who hadn't stopped talking about himself all night. He can't have been that interested in my story since the only time he'd shut up was to take another drink. And there was still a glimmer of something in his eyes that I couldn't read; not that I could judge him for that. I didn't exactly enter into this thinking he'd be my Prince Charming, and I certainly hadn't been honest. The only things I'd told him that were true were where I lived and that I worked in a coffee shop. Didn't even tell him which one. Even the personality traits I showed him weren't accurate. This guy wouldn't have lasted two minutes with me under normal circumstances, and aside from my little blip when he first spoke to me, I'd been nothing but polite and interested in his bullshit.

Well, there was that moment when I pushed my boobs in his face, but, like I said… desperate times.

"I got a lot of stories," I told him, smiling. "But none of them are going to be told tonight." We stopped as we reached my apartment building. "This is me."

Finn stood in front of me, his arms hanging loosely at his sides. I couldn't stop looking at them, wondering if he was going to reach out for me, make a move. "I'd like to hear some of those stories sometime."

Thank God. The evening hadn't been a total waste of time. I'd got him hooked; at least enough to want to see me again. The game was nowhere near over yet.

I smiled up at him. My smile was genuine this time; not because I was eager to hear him bragging again, but because now the plan was really in motion.

Finn's hands found my waist and he pulled me to him. A warm, tingling sensation shot through me, and when he leaned down, his mouth close to mine, my heart stuttered.

That's repulsion, right? It had to be. The man was a first-class moron. Apart from that time he said I was a different kind of pretty. That was kinda sweet. *He's still a bent cop. He still is the most likely person to have helped plant the gun at Matteo's house. Don't Get. Sucked. In.* Again, the danger of this plan hit me like a baseball bat to the gut, but I wasn't as afraid as I should have been. *In fact…*

My tongue slipped out to moisten my suddenly dry lips as Finn stared into my eyes. I felt like I was being hypnotized by those pools of blueness, and his already gravelly voice turned huskier than ever. "Invite me in."

The words fluttered over my skin and I nodded, unable to speak.

I wasn't sure what the hell was happening, but I knew I had to go with it. More worrying was that I wanted to. A huge part of me wanted to hear that sexy as hell voice whispering in my ear. Wanted to feel his lips and his hands on me again.

I barely remembered the walk up the stairs to my apartment—I was too busy being concerned about the fucked up way my mind worked—but as soon as we were inside, I dropped my bag and keys on the floor as Finn slammed me against the door, stealing my breath, his hands pressing into my hips and my arms reaching up and winding around his neck. His lips found mine and I let out an involuntary moan, as if I'd been waiting for this moment all night.

Hypnotism. It had to be. There was no other reasonable explanation for the way my body reacted to him. No reasonable explanation why I could barely breathe as his tongue danced with mine, and why I couldn't seem to get close enough to him. His kisses left my lips and trailed across my jawline, then slowly, torturously, down my neck. My eyelids fluttered shut as my whole body sagged against him. I moved my hands down his strong arms and slipped them around his waist, tugging at his shirt until it untucked from pants, then snaked my hands upwards, touching his bare skin. He let out a soft groan and dug his fingers harder into my hips before sliding his hands underneath my top. My hips pushed against his as his fingertips grazed the edge of my bra.

"I need to ask you something," Finn said, his breath tickling the skin on my shoulder.

"What is it?"

His lips moved back to mine, kissing me one more time then he pulled back just a fraction so his lips hovered over mine. "How far are you planning to take this? Darcy."

And just like that, the magic was broken. Reality came screaming in and I froze. *Darcy. He called me Darcy.*

His deep laugh shook me from my trance and I dropped my arms from around him, placed my hands on his chest, and shoved him backward.

"You didn't think I knew who you are? That I didn't know that the first time I saw you in the bar? Little tip for you; if you want to trick a police officer, it's better that you're not in the courthouse looking devastated the day a particular verdict is given."

The glint of amusement in his eyes made me want to knee him in the nuts, and my own eyes narrowed. "I was barely noticeable amongst all the people in there because I knew it would come down to this. I knew I'd have to do something fucking crazy to find out the truth."

"Little newsflash for you; girls like you are not designed to blend into a crowd. Also, we do these things called investigations. Helps us find the murderer. And while researching who the victim's friends were, your name and face popped up more than once. You were even on the suspect list."

"Bullshit. If you knew who I was, why wasn't I ever questioned?"

"Because the murder weapon was found at Matteo's house," he said, as if talking to a small child.

"So? Anyone could have put it there. *I* could have put it there."

"Did you?"

I placed my hands on my hips. "Listen, Detective, you may think I'm an idiot, but do you really think I'd get this far involved if I'd killed her myself?" After glaring at him for a moment, I straightened up, ready to walk away, but he stepped into me again, grabbing my wrists and pinning them above my head. I inhaled sharply at his fast move and his closeness. God, he smelled good; like beer and cologne, and I subtly breathed in his scent.

He leaned in toward me with a cruel smirk. "Sweetheart, I've seen things you wouldn't believe, and that includes people doing dangerous things to frame someone for a crime they committed."

"Things like planting evidence so the wrong man goes to jail?"

He nodded. "I gotta admit though, this is the first time I've ever had a woman trying to screw a confession out of me."

"Well," I said, tilting my head to the side, scorn dripping from my words, "you can forget about that now. Sorry to disappoint you."

"Me?" He laughed. "Please. If anyone's disappointed here, it's you." I opened my mouth to protest but he silenced me with a kiss and, to my annoyance, my body softened as his lips burned a path across my cheek. With his mouth by my ear, he breathed, "Admit it. This would have been a double bonus for you if your little plan had worked."

My own breathing had become ragged with his movements. His grip on my wrists was still tight, and I had to focus hard to stop my voice from quivering. "You wish. It may have escaped your attention, but I was bored as hell this evening while you were chirping on about how much of a great cop you are."

His lips stilled on my neck. He looked up at me for a second, unmoving, then dropped my hands and stepped away from me, shrugging. "If you insist."

The chill I felt as his body moved away hit me hard but I pulled back my shoulders, trying to pretend he wasn't right. Inexplicably so, since he *had* been dull for three quarters of the night.

Oh God. I'd blown it. On the first day, I'd blown it, and

now he knew I was onto him–onto *them*. What was I supposed to do now? What would happen to me? Any desire I'd felt for Finn slithered away as fear replaced it, filling my veins with ice.

Shit. What the hell had I been thinking? I wasn't cut out for this; I was coffee house girl. Sure, I had a degree in journalism, but I'd turned into coffee house girl. I was never undercover investigator material and, even though I'd done my homework, done everything in my power not to be caught–or so I'd thought–I'd still screwed it up.

"Don't look so worried, sweetheart."

I shifted my regard to Finn, who had perched himself on the arm of my couch, his smirk still firmly in place. "So, what are you going to do to me now? Should I expect to find a dead body in the trunk of my car? Drugs planted in my work locker?"

"You really do have a bad image of me, don't you?"

"What do you expect?" I took a few steps toward him. "I know you know what I know. I know you do. And if you know then there's a real good chance you helped set Matteo up."

"So, what was your plan? Were you going to record my confession on your phone?"

Actually, I hadn't thought that far ahead. Hell, I'd thought we had at least a few weeks before that became an issue.

"Look, *Darcy*. You're looking at the wrong guy. I had nothing to do with any set-up. But… I do think you're right."

My eyes narrowed. "What?"

"I think Torres was set up, I just don't know by whom."

"But when you took the stand, you said–"

"I told the truth."

"The truth? If you didn't think Matteo was guilty, you should have said so! Your statement helped get him locked up!"

Finn stood up, stepping closer to me again. "What was I supposed to say? Huh? I couldn't take to the stand and say I was there when the murder weapon was discovered but I didn't think Matteo was guilty. His blood was on the goddamn gun!"

"You had more information! You knew the one thing that nobody was talking about."

That Rebecca was having a fling with the brother of a cop. Matteo had refused to tell the cops that Rebeca had been cheating at first because, in spite of the fact that her fuck buddy was the most likely murderer, he loved her so much that he didn't want her name dragged through the mud. In the end, though the police got into her phone to look for more evidence against Matteo, and it was Drake who had found calls and messages from a Dylan Miller. However, when it came to the trial, the prosecution had denied the evidence was relevant and argued that it isn't cool to accuse a murder victim of being a whore. Apparently, the corruption wasn't just within the police force—it ran way higher. The "good guys" prosecuting a murderer couldn't have corrupt cops being uncovered. Besides, Dylan Miller had an airtight alibi—provided by none other than his big brother, Al. In the end, that whole line of investigation got thrown out, leaving Matteo the only person in the frame.

From what I'd figured out, Dylan Miller was an asshole, and the only reason he'd never been in jail was because Al had been covering for him for years. Prior to Rebecca's death, Dylan's crimes had mainly been drug related. He was tall, dark, and tattooed, but he was also violent and she was married. I had no idea what had possessed her to get involved with someone so dangerous.

Ha. Pot. Kettle. Because trying to bed a cop for information was a really smart idea.

A familiar feeling of anger mixed with guilt rushed through me again. I couldn't help it. I was still so mad at Rebecca for cheating on Matteo. She'd destroyed my best friend with her selfish actions, and he'd still been willing to forgive her even though she didn't deserve it. She didn't deserve *him*. But she'd lost her life. What she'd done certainly didn't warrant her being killed.

Finn's eyes lowered to the floor. "You don't know shit, Darcy. And honestly, it'd be better for you if it stayed that way."

"What does that mean? And, seriously? You think I should just let this drop? That I should forget that Matteo's in jail for something he didn't do?"

"Why are you so desperate to help him?" Finn looked up at me again. "You got a thing for him or something?"

I rolled my eyes. If I'd had a dollar for every time someone had asked about my friendship with Matteo, I'd have been able to afford to hire a lawyer who could actually help him. Shaking my head, I walked toward Finn and sat down on the arm of the couch he'd just risen from. "Why does everyone find it so hard to believe that a man and a woman can be just friends?"

Finn's stare ran up and down the length of my body. "Well, no offence, but friendship ain't the first thing I think of when I look at you. And you met Matteo when you were... what? Eighteen?"

"You've really done your homework, haven't you? Yes. I was eighteen when I met him. What difference does that make?"

"Oh, come on. Everyone's horny in college. You're hot, and I have it on good authority that Torres is considered a good-looking guy. You never once hooked up?"

We never had sex, but we did make out one night after drinking too much at a college party. Once. Real early on. It didn't last long and we both agreed we were way better off as buddies. Of course, that was none of Drake's damn business. I shook my head. "You're getting off track. All you need to know is that Matteo and I are friends. Best friends. What did you mean when you said I don't know shit?"

Finn straightened up his shirt; it was still rumpled from where I'd clung to him while he kissed me. My lips tingled just from the memory.

"All you need to know is this is over, kid." He turned to me, his face serious. "You tried, and in spite of me mocking you, you might be the kind of girl who could have gotten to my deepest, darkest secrets. But I've got nothing for you. Not about this."

He started to walk toward the door and I cried out, "So now what? You tell me you think Matteo's innocent but you're still gonna walk away? Let him stay where he is while whoever killed Rebecca is out there?"

"I'm working on it, okay? I'm working on it."

Chapter 3
Finn

Well, shit. That evening in the bar could be summed with these simple words: *That didn't go as planned.* I hadn't exactly known what Miss Darcy Ryan was planning when she started talking to me in the bar, but I'd known for a while that she was up to something. I have to admit, I admired her spirit. A girl willing to fuck a stranger to get her best friend out of jail? Well, that was the kind of loyalty I didn't see too often. All I'd wanted to do was find out how much she knew. About Torres and his wife and what she'd been getting up to behind his back. Turned out she knew less than half of the entire messed up situation, and call me insane–hey, I must have been for even caring about the crazy bitch who wanted to trick me–but I wanted to keep it that way. She was in over her head the second she decided to try to solve this thing herself.

As I entered my own apartment, just two blocks from hers, I threw my keys down on the table by the door, took off my shoes, and headed straight to the fridge to grab another beer. God knows I needed it. I'd popped off the top and swallowed half the damn bottle before I took a deep breath and leaned back against the kitchen counter.

I couldn't let her get mixed up in any of this. I might have only just met her, but there were two things I'd figured out fast. One, she was loyal to the point of insanity. And two, she wasn't kidding when she'd said she and Torres were best friends. There were photos of her with him and his tramp of a wife all over her living room. Okay, there were two–further proof that she hadn't been nearly as ready for me as she thought. If she had been, she'd have put them out of sight. I chuckled to myself. Darcy was smart, but she hadn't considered every possible ending to the evening. Didn't cross her mind that she'd take me home the first time she met me.

I guess she underestimated my charm.

From what I could see, there were no photos of any family anywhere around. Just ones of her and the Torres', and a couple more of her with some female friends that had been taken in bars.

So, if anything happened to her... with Matteo behind bars... who would miss her?

Maybe that was why she was so reckless. Without her best friend, maybe she figured she had nothing left to lose.

Fuck.

I'd left her letting her know I was working on figuring this mess out, but that wouldn't be enough for her. It just wouldn't. And if she uncovered the truth, there was a good chance she'd end up dead.

I slammed my bottle down on the table, snarling in frustration. I should have just left her alone. Should have stayed away. Although, that wouldn't have made a difference. Not when she'd already made up her mind to try to get to me.

And she *had* got to me. I ain't just talking about meeting her. I'd watched her every time I saw her in that bar. I'd spotted her in the courtroom, even though she'd tried to hide behind her long, dark hair. She had a vulnerability about her, even though she played the tough girl. Something about her told me she'd been through some shit and, for whatever reason, I didn't want her to go through anymore.

Didn't hurt that she was beautiful. I mean, kissing her? Not the roughest thing I'd ever done in my life. The hard part was stopping. I hadn't been able to resist mocking her, but hey, I never claimed I wasn't an asshole. I could tell she wasn't dumb, but trying to take me on? Not a good idea.

23

I felt my cellphone vibrate in my pocket and I pulled it out to look at the message on the screen.

Let me help you. Please. Whatever you need. I'll do anything.

I sighed. "Oh hell."

I typed back: **Darcy, stay out of it. It's dangerous. This isn't a game.**

Within seconds, she answered: **No offence, but I'm still not sure I trust you. You either let me help you or I'll find another way.**

Another growl escaped me and I hit the button to call her. This damn woman was going to be a pain in my ass. The moment the call connected, I didn't give her a chance to speak. "Darcy, I'm serious. Do not get tangled up in this mess. You have to let me deal with this."

"I don't even know what *this* is. What are you keeping from me, Drake?"

"I can't discuss the case with you. I've already said more than I should have."

I should have lied. Told her I thought Matteo was guilty and carried on investigating on my own, but my head was still reeling from that damn kiss, and in spite of all the reasons it was wrong… I wanted to see her again. Now, with a slightly clearer head, I knew I shouldn't have given her my number before I left her place. Shouldn't have led her on at all. Should have walked her to her apartment, kissed her on the cheek, and gone home to jerk off while thinking about how it would have felt to have those perfect, plump lips all over me.

"You haven't said enough!" she hissed, and the sound of her voice combined with the thoughts I had about her made my dick twitch. "What do you know?"

"You have to stop pushing." I adjusted my jeans and tried to think of something, anything else to redirect the flow of blood back to my brain while I dealt with her. "Do you understand what we're talking about here? We're talking about a murderer, Darcy. The person who killed your friend. If you get too close, you'll be next."

"Then you'll have to protect me, won't you?"

Her voice had softened and I closed my eyes, breathing deeply for a few seconds. She sure as shit wasn't making this easy for me. But if I left her? If I turned my back on her? She wasn't kidding when she said she'd keep digging around. She'd already showed me what she was prepared to do to get to the truth. What would be next? Would she be willing to get into bed with Dylan Miller if it would get Torres out of jail?

I muttered a curse word under my breath. "Tomorrow. I have the day off. Can I meet you somewhere?"

"I get off work at four. You wanna meet me there?"

"Fine. But, Darcy? Once I tell you this stuff, I'm not gonna be able to take it back. And you're not gonna want to hear it. Do you get that?"

"I need to know," she said quietly. "I need to."

Chapter 4
Darcy

My Saturday shifts usually flew by, but this one? It dragged on for an eternity. Seemed like every customer wanted the most complex coffees known to man, and took approximately seven years each to decide that. It was a surprise to me that I got through the day without screwing up anyone's order since coffee was the last thing on my mind.

When Finn picked me up from work at four, my nerves were shot. I'd checked my appearance in the mirror before I left, and although I'd managed to maintain a tidy appearance, my eyes didn't look right. They looked pale, and my whole face was a little haggard.

I'd thought of nothing but what Finn might reveal to me from the second he hung up the phone the night before. *You're not gonna want to hear it.* But what could it possibly be? I'd already figured out Dylan was the one who'd killed Rebecca, and that he'd relied on his big brother to help him cover it up. Or at least that was the obvious way it went down.

I had been wrong about Finn, though. At least, I hoped so. Everything about him had screamed *corruption*. I couldn't explain it. There was just something in his demeanor, something in his arrogance that said, *'I can do what I want and get away with it, and there's nothing you can do to stop me.'* Having spent some time with him, sure he was smug, but he wasn't corrupt... probably. I wasn't ready to let my guard right down around him, but I had got into his car and let him take me to a coffee shop on the outskirts of the city.

He sat opposite me at a table at the back of the trendy diner. It was a far cry from the down to earth vibe of the bar we'd met in, and from the coffee shop I worked in. This one was decked out in browns and creams, and the chairs were huge and squidgy; the kind you can sink into.

Now we were finally there, I wasn't sure I wanted to hear what he had to say at all. His hands were linked together on the table in front of him, his coffee cup slightly to the side. My hands gripped my mug so hard I was surprised it didn't shatter. His face was stony, serious, but it wasn't that that scared me. There was something like sympathy in his eyes. Something that told me he knew that whatever he was going to say would hurt me. I closed my eyes for a moment, trying to brace myself for the impact of his words.

"Okay," I began. "Please can you tell me what the hell is going on?"

Finn stared at me for a moment longer then puffed out a breath, running a hand through his hair. "There's really no gentle way to say this, Darcy. I wish there was, but–"

"Just tell me, dammit!" I wasn't mad at him, but the tension had been slowly killing me all day and I needed answers. I didn't care for sympathy. Only the truth.

"Okay. Okay. Rebecca Torres was… let's say she had a thing for cops."

My head dropped to one side. "What?"

"She waited tables at that Italian place not far from your coffee house, right?"

I nodded. "Yeah."

"Some of our guys go there to pick up take out, and sometimes we go there to hang out because they make great pizza and serve good beer. Rebecca was well-known. And by that I mean, sometimes she'd slip her phone number in with our orders."

I raised an eyebrow. "You're kidding, right?"

His head slowly shook from side to side. "Nope. I can name at least four other guys she gave her number to. Not including me."

My eyebrows rose higher. "No. There's no way. You're lying."

He had to be mistaken. Yeah, she had an affair, but she was never leaving Matteo. She loved him. That was what had been contained in those text messages to Dylan that he'd found on Rebecca's phone. Messages saying she loved her husband and would never leave him. And if she loved him, why would she have been giving her number out to every guy she met? It's one thing having a fling, but to be looking to set up others…?

"I told you you wouldn't like it. She might have been having a thing with Dylan Miller, but she was screwing other cops too. She approached me many times."

I wanted him to be lying so bad, but he didn't break my gaze for a second. He looked almost apologetic, and I said, "Did you ever take her up on her offers?"

"No." He leaned forward across the table as if to tell me a secret. "I prefer my women single."

Finn's eyes flicked up and down the top half of my body, the way he'd done the night before, and I felt my heart speed up.

Blinking, I said, "So… what? You want me to believe one of my best friends was out blowing cops in her spare time?"

He chuckled, that throaty laugh that made goose bumps pop up on my skin, as he sat back in his chair. "She *was* blowing cops in her spare time. She was practically at their beck and call. I couldn't tell you why, or what the appeal was for her. Maybe it was the uniform. Chicks dig uniforms."

Ignoring his comment, I tried to process what he was telling me. If that was really true, if Rebecca had been out sleeping with cops, was Finn trying to say that Dylan was only one in a long list of possible suspects? And if she'd been screwing cops, who knew who else she'd been doing it with? Finn could only speak for the ones he knew about. Maybe it wasn't just cops she was into. Perhaps she just liked sleeping with anyone.

"I don't understand this." I picked up the napkin from beside my mug and began running it through my fingers. "I don't know what the hell kind of image she was portraying when she was at work, but that's not… I mean… she wasn't like that."

"She was flirty every time I saw her. I thought it was just something she was doing to earn extra tips. A lot of waitresses flirt with customers for that reason, but she was more than flirty. Some of the guys-" he trailed off and I stared at him.

"What?"

"She sent some photos. Of… you know."

Oh God, this was getting worse by the second. I wrinkled my nose at the thought of the girl I thought I knew sending pictures of her boobs and who knew what else to random guys. Rebecca… okay. Perhaps it was time to exercise a little honesty. When I first met her, I didn't like her. In fact, I thought she had an attitude problem. She was brash, and I thought Matteo was out of his damn mind getting involved with her. Over time, though, I got to know her a little more. Found out the attitude was more like a front to keep away people who weren't strong enough to handle her. She had opinions, and God help anyone who told her she was wrong. But not once did I suspect she was a cheat, and sure as hell not someone who'd be sending out slutty photos.

"I can't even…" I shook my head. "I don't want to hear any more about that. Do you know how she went from hooking up with cops to having a full blown affair with Dylan?"

Finn sighed, shaking his head again. "I don't know how that happened, but I do know she met him around six months ago because I was there that night. She was pretty into him but I don't know why she wanted him over any of the other guys she hooked up with. Dylan Miller is a psychopath. He's been in a bunch of trouble for violent behavior, from smashing bottles over people's heads to much more sick and twisted shit. I'll spare you the details. But he's always managed to avoid getting jail time, thanks to his big brother, Al."

"So, even though Rebecca was involved with half the damn police force, you still think Dylan killed her?"

He nodded. "He's the most likely one. Some of my guys have questionable morals but none of them are killers. I think Dylan wanted her to leave Torres, and when she wouldn't, he killed her knowing Al would do anything to keep him out of jail. And–bonus–Torres would get the blame."

I sat in silence for a moment, letting his words sink in. Rebecca Torres. Not the faithful devoted wife she appeared, but a serial cheater. And messing around with a guy who sounded severely unhinged had got her killed. Sure, I'd guessed the latter part of this equation, but I was still in shock from finding out what she was really like.

But why? Matteo was the perfect guy. He was good-looking and fun and smart. He worshipped her, gave her everything she wanted. Maybe that was the problem. Maybe having everything she wanted didn't provide her with enough of a challenge, and she wanted something more. It was a fucked up way of thinking, but weren't some women into that kind of thing? Having it all and still wanting more?

I felt my nails digging into the palms of my hands as the truth finally settled in. How stupid we all were. How totally blinded. And the worst part? She was dead so I couldn't even ask her why. Why she cheated on the man who would have walked through fire for her.

"I'm sorry." Finn's voice brought me back to reality. "You wanted to know."

"You were right. Now I wish I didn't."

He reached over and rested his hands over mine until they slowly unclenched. "Darcy, I know you want to get Torres out of jail, but I need you to leave this to me. You don't know how dangerous Dylan is."

I glared at him. "He killed someone. That's a pretty good fucking indication."

A small smile flickered across Finn's lips but it faded as quickly as it had appeared. "Let me handle it."

"How? How are you going to prove this?"

"I can't tell you that. I just need you to trust me."

"Trust you? I don't even know you."

He smirked. "You're here, aren't you? If you didn't trust me, you wouldn't have got into my car."

"I'm here because I wanted to know what you know. And now I do…" I shrugged. "Now I need to figure out what to do with the information."

I was totally bullshitting. I had no idea what I was supposed to do with what he'd told me, but when he leaned forward and gripped my hands again, I knew I'd rattled him.

"Darcy, I swear to God. I will lock you in your own apartment if you don't promise to leave this alone."

It was my turn to smirk. "Is this genuine concern for me, Detective Drake?"

His hands slid to my wrists, gripping them tight like handcuffs. "That, or maybe I just like the idea of being in control of you." His voice had deepened, the huskiness more prominent, causing a shiver to run through me.

"I got news for you, buddy." I leaned in closer to him so my mouth was just an inch from his. "Nobody controls me."

Finn's eyes narrowed, growing darker by the second. "Listen, you crazy bitch. This ain't up for discussion. I admire your dedication, but I won't let you put your life at risk."

"My life. My decision."

Without warning, Finn captured my lips with his, cutting off both my breath and my thoughts. *Okay, maybe I'd be okay with him controlling me.* I just wasn't going to let him know that.

I dipped my tongue out, moistening my bottom lip while keeping my eyes on him. "I'll tell you what. I'll give you a week. If you've got nothing for me in seven days, I'm doing this my way."

Chapter 5
Finn

I rested my head against my desk, my temples aching. I wasn't supposed to be in my office on my day off, but it was the only place I could think clearly. Sounds stupid, I know. I spent so much time there, you'd think home would be a better place to get my shit together, but there was something about my workspace that grounded me. Maybe it was the scent of stale coffee in the air that reminded me how exhausting yet rewarding the job was. Maybe it was having my evidence board crammed with clues about my latest case that reminded me that what I did was worthwhile. Or maybe it was just because being in that place gave me a sense of purpose. There wasn't a whole lot going on in my life besides work. Hadn't been in years. Partly through choice. I was a cop through and through. Felt like it had been born into me. Solving crimes was what I'd wanted to do, and since my parents were drug-addled criminals, it only motivated me more. I didn't want to be like them. Countless years in jail that saw me dumped with families that weren't my own, not to mention the fact that their addictions had driven them both to a very early grave. I didn't much care for their type. Sure, addiction sucks, but at some point in their lives, they made a decision. To use for the first time, and to keep on doing it until they had nothing left.

But enough about that. I had a whole new unofficial case to deal with, and a barista with absolutely no concern for her own life to keep safe.

That woman. She was doing strange things to my brain and other parts of my body. It wasn't just that she was hot. And she wasn't just *hot*–she was pretty. Sexy. But it was the fire in her eyes that kept me thinking about her. Maybe deep down she was just a young woman playing the part of an adult who was ready to take on the world. Maybe that *was* a part of her. But that inner determination she had, that loyalty? That wasn't fake. She truly was willing to put her ass on the line for the sake of her friend.

But I couldn't let her. Before she came along, finding out the truth behind Rebecca Torres' murder had been an ongoing thing that happened around the cases I was supposed to be working on. Now, it was a matter of urgency. And I didn't have a damn clue where to start – not within the time frame she'd given me.

The investigation had been a joke from start to finish. I knew–we all knew–Rebecca had a reputation, and we all knew she'd been getting it on with Dylan for months. We also knew he was possessive and fucking insane. The other cops seemed almost relieved when the gun appeared at Matteo's place, like they wouldn't have to face the fact that someone they knew might have killed her.

The biggest problem for me at first was figuring out why Matteo Torres' blood was on that gun. Nobody questioned it. Well, his lawyer did. But to the jury? Weapon found in suspect's house with his blood on it? Add to that the CCTV footage of Rebecca and Matteo arguing at a club they attended the night of her death. Case freaking closed. And maybe that should have been enough for me too. But my gut instinct told me something wasn't right. A little digging showed me Torres had once been arrested for a suspected DUI. He hadn't been drinking, but his friend had. Blood was taken from them both and he was found to be clean, but that meant that his blood was still locked away, and people in my department–people such as Al Miller–had access.

But why would he get this involved? Al did a lot to keep his brother out of trouble, but framing someone for murder? His moral compass wasn't so fucked up that he'd go this far.

Right?

Hell if I knew. Hell if I knew anything anymore.

The only thing I knew for sure was that I had to figure it out. And fast.

My head snapped up when I heard a knock on my office door. *Fuck.* I raised my hand and signaled for Al to come in.

"Hey, buddy," I said, sitting up straight and flicking my brain into work mode and my expression into neutral. At least I hoped I had. One thing I was good at was keeping a stoic expression; I had to be. Couldn't have emotion giving people any clues about what I was thinking, and I especially couldn't afford to let Al get any insights since I wasn't sure I could trust him anymore.

Al Miller outsized me in every way. Taller, built bigger; he was actually a little intimidating to those who didn't know him. In spite of his misguided tendency to cover up his brother's messes, he was a good cop. We'd always worked well together, and he'd saved my ass on more than one occasion.

He almost filled the entire doorframe as he stood, regarding me while awkwardly shifting from one foot to the other. This wasn't a sign of anything unusual. Al was always slightly awkward. Probably a side effect of covering up so much of this brother's shit. Even though most of us knew about it. Fuck. What kind of people were we that we let this slide for so long?

There's a big difference between getting someone off a charge for a scuffle in a bar and covering up a murder.

I tried to shrug off the knowledge that he'd gotten away with more than the occasional scuffle and fixed my focus back on Al.

"What are you doing here?" he asked. "You know you *are* allowed to use your days off? You're looking tired, man."

I nodded. "I know. I was at a loose end and I wanted to try and get a little more done on the Dallison case." I held up the file in front of me that I'd put there for a situation just like this. Rule number one of sneaking around: always have a cover story.

"You got anything?"

"Not yet." I placed the file back down and sighed. "We need to pull some of the witnesses back in for further questioning. There's something missing."

Al's lips curled upwards at the corners. "Right. I'm on it. But you need to go home, Drake. You're running yourself into the ground being here every hour God sends."

`His stance relaxed a little and he raised his eyebrows. I shook my head as I looked at him, seeing him as the guy I'd seen him as for the last few years. My colleague. My buddy. Before I could answer him, another figure appeared in my doorway. The smaller frame of another colleague, Lieutenant Chris Sampson. When he saw me, he rolled his eyes.

"Drake, seriously? Get your ass out of here until tomorrow. We ain't paying you overtime, so go home. That's an order."

With an eye roll of my own at the abrasive asshole, I stood up. "Yes, sir."

With a sigh, I grabbed my jacket from the back of my chair. If I wasn't going to make any progress with the case, I'd go grab a drink at Midnight Rodeo. A few beers had never helped me think more clearly, but what the hell. Anything was better than going back to my apartment and staring at my own four walls.

Chapter 6
Darcy

Tick, tock.

As I lay on my bed a little more than twenty-four hours after Finn took me home after our coffee date, that was the only sound I heard. Each tick was another second Matteo was behind bars for no reason. Each minute was another sixty seconds he sat inside a cold, empty cell. Each hour was another sixty minutes of his life wasted.

I'd given Finn a week to figure out the truth, which may have been a lot of pressure on him because I'd made him think I had a plan B. Hopefully. Really, the pressure was on me because if he didn't come up with the goods, I had nothing. Finn Drake had been my only focus. He'd seemed like the most obvious person to have helped set up Matteo, and now he was… well, maybe not on my side, but he wasn't who I thought he was. Probably.

I let out a small groan into the empty room. I still wasn't ready to trust him yet, but man, he'd gotten under my skin. That was precisely *why* I didn't trust him. I'd had my defenses up as high as they could go, but as soon as he'd kissed me, all bets were off.

There had to be something seriously wrong inside my head. I'm not stupid. I was fully aware that I'd have to put my morals on ice for this little mission, and I was desperate enough to help Matteo to do it. But I was happier when I thought Drake was a corrupt cop, because that way, I didn't have to deal with any of the questions in my head. Now, I was more than halfway sure he was decent, and more than that, I was actually relying on him to help me. I never wanted that. I'd spent most of my life not depending on anyone; I didn't want to start now. Especially not over something this important.

I glanced at the clock. Matteo would be calling soon. I'd wanted to wait until my next visit to tell him how things had gone but he'd insisted on calling me. Mostly, I think, to make sure I was okay. That I hadn't gotten in over my head already. The problem was, we couldn't speak freely. All of his calls were recorded; there would be no privacy. How was I supposed to tell him anything without raising suspicion?

And what about the things I'd found out about Rebecca? Even face to face, there was no way I could tell him she was cheating on him with more than one person. Nobody else in the world knew how hard his heart had broken when he found out his college sweetheart was fucking someone else. To tell him there was more than one guy would have been cruel.

But what about honesty? I was trying to find out who Rebecca's real killer was. What if it wasn't Miller? What if it *was* one of the others? Wouldn't it be better to tell him upfront than have to explain it was someone else later?

I huffed out a sigh and pressed my face into my pillow to muffle the scream of frustration that was desperate to escape my lips.

Why us? Why Matteo? Why, just for once, couldn't my life not be a gigantic fuck up? I may have never been the little girl who dreamed of finding her Prince Charming and skipping off into the sunset–that dream was for kids with happy childhoods–but I'd expected that, one day, life would even out. That I'd reach my quota of crap that could be thrown at me, and things would be better.

As the phone beside my bed started to ring, I took a deep breath before picking it up and answering. After the usual far too familiar recorded message telling me I had a call from the prison, I waited until I heard Matteo's tentative voice.

"Hey," I said. "How are you?"

"Better now I've heard your voice." The sigh he let out told me exactly how much he'd been stewing over my meeting with Finn.

"I'm fine," I said, with an air of soft reassurance. "I'm fine."

"Is there anything you need to tell me?"

I paused for a second, trying to work out how to put into words everything that had happened since I stumbled upon Finn Drake.

"Darcy?"

"So… you remember that blind date I said I was going on?"

"Uh-huh." Tension crept back into Matteo's voice.

"It was better than I thought it would be. The guy was… different."

"Different how?"

"Well, he came off real arrogant at first. I wanted to leave after twenty minutes but I gave him a chance." *I stayed out of sheer desperation to help you.* "He's really not who I thought he was."

I gave Matteo a moment to let my words sink in, hoping he understood what I was telling him. Okay, so I hadn't one hundred percent made up my mind about Drake, but I had to at least let Matteo know that Drake might not be our guy.

"You sure?" he asked.

"Ninety percent. I'm going to see him again."

"Darcy, you…" he paused, and I knew he'd almost reacted the way he would have if we'd been in the same room. With words that shouldn't be spoken over a recorded call. "I'm pleased for you. But I don't want you to get hurt. I want you to be one hundred and fifty percent sure he's the kind of guy you need in your life."

"I know. But to figure that out, I have to spend more time with him. I promise I won't rush into anything."

"Not your strong point."

I chuckled because he was right, and that became even more true when it came to his freedom. But I knew in advance I would be playing the long game with Finn, and as much as I wanted to move this along quickly, I had to find the strength to keep my cool. For all our sakes.

"I can do this, Matty. You need to trust me."

"I do trust you. You're about the only one I do trust these days."

My stomach knotted at his words. They served to remind me just how much my actions could affect him. It wasn't as if that knowledge ever really left me; my heart was heavy from the second I woke up until the moment I fell asleep. Knowing he'd placed all his hopes in me, even though it scared him as much as it scared me, was a huge burden to carry. I was never going to betray him the way Rebecca did, but the fear that I might not be able to do what I set out to do constantly kept me on edge.

"So, what else is new?" Matteo asked, because there was really nowhere else for that conversation to go until we saw each other again.

"Not much. Work. Home. Same old."

"I'm worried about you, Darcy," Matteo said, after a slight pause. "Just because I'm stuck in here, that doesn't mean you can't go on living your life. You're not the one who got a life sentence."

I groaned. "Matty, please. Not this again. You know how I feel. I'm trying, okay? I'm trying to do normal stuff and socialize but it doesn't feel right. It hasn't felt right since you were arrested. It's not… it's not the same without you."

Throughout college and after, Matteo had been the best person to party with. Rebecca too… *before*. Damn, I couldn't shake the questions about her. Had she been a cheat the whole time she'd been with Matteo? Or was it just the lure of a cop uniform and the thrill of screwing a bad guy?

Unaware of the thoughts racing through my skull, Matteo said, "I'm gonna need you to try harder. It's bad enough that I'm in here, but you? You're free and you need to enjoy it. If I get out of here, I'm never going to take my freedom for granted again."

"There's no *if*," I said firmly. "You're getting out and we're going to… I don't know. We'll go somewhere."

"We'll party in Europe like we always wanted to." I could almost hear the smile in his voice, and it made me smile a little too.

"London. Paris. Amsterdam. They won't know what's hit them."

Matteo laughed; a sound I missed with every fiber of my being, and my heart ached for my best friend. For the fear that I might let him down and he'd be left serving a sentence that wasn't his to serve.

Chapter 7
Darcy

"Thank the sweet Lord that shift is over." I huffed out a sigh as I tugged my apron off in the staff area of the coffee shop I worked in. Honestly, it wasn't the shift that was the problem, it was me. Since talking to Matteo the night before, my stress levels had accelerated, and I hadn't heard from Finn in way too long. That meant he was either ignoring my threat to take this thing on alone, or he'd decided my protection wasn't his concern.

Or he's as sick as you first thought and it would simply be easier for him if someone permanently silenced you.

A shudder ran through me at the thought.

"And it's only Monday," Amelia, my co-worker said as she dropped her bag down and shrugged off her jacket. "Not that it makes a difference to those of us who work every hour God sends."

I threw her a sympathetic smile. Amelia was soon to turn thirty, and she busted her ass at the coffee house to support her four-year-old son after his dad decided that having sex with his secretary was more appealing than family life. Her parents helped her out, sitting for the kid, but Amelia refused any handouts. She was, however, planning to make sure her deadbeat ex-boyfriend didn't shirk his financial responsibilities when it came to their son. It was the least he could do after being such a good for nothing dirtbag.

"Any chance of a night on the town this weekend?" I asked, handing her a clean apron from the pile that rested on the shelf just behind me.

I was trying hard to keep Matteo's advice on board. Maybe blowing off a little steam was exactly what I needed and, even if it was only Amelia and me, it would be better than sitting at home pretending to watch TV.

Amelia's face twisted into a doubtful grimace. "I don't know. I'm on the late shift on Friday and I'm covering for Kristian for a couple hours on Saturday afternoon. My parents have been great taking care of Mason but I don't want to take advantage."

I nodded, trying to keep the disappointment from showing on my face. "I understand. But let's try to go out soon."

"I didn't say no." Amelia smiled. "I could use a night on the town too. Leave it with me. I'll see what I can do."

I grinned at her enthusiasm and we high-fived each other as we left the staff area and went out into the coffee shop. Amelia left ahead of me, and she stopped abruptly, gasping as she walked into a tall, slim, and all-too-familiar man wearing a gray suit, a crisp white shirt, and a dark blue tie, as if he'd just finished work.

"Dude, seriously," she said, looking up at him. "You need to stand somewhere other than the door to the staff room. You'll give someone a freaking heart attack." Her hand covered her own heart at the shock of smacking into him. As her eyes fell on him, she added, "I know you."

Finn fixed her with a smug grin—the one I'd grown pretty accustomed to lately—his eyes sparkling with amusement. "I'm sure you do. You probably remember me from Midnight Rodeo. Darcy's been stalking me there for quite some time."

My eyes narrowed as Amelia whipped her head around to look at me. "What do you want, Drake?" I asked.

Amelia raised her eyebrows and laughed then slipped out from between us to start her shift, leaving me alone with the arrogant detective.

"I'm taking you out for dinner," he told me, in a way that suggested I had no choice in the matter.

I started to walk past him. "I'm sure you think you are, but I have plans with a hot bubble bath and several glasses of wine."

I heard his footsteps behind me. "That could work."

With a sarcastic chuckle, I said, "You're not invited."

As I paused at the door to let some customers into the still busy coffee house, Finn pressed his body against my back and whispered in my ear, "You sure? You seem tense, Darcy. I'm real good at relieving tension."

He spoke every word slowly, and each one traveled directly to my core, much to my irritation. That damn husky voice was fast becoming my kryptonite. Without flinching, I turned to him, looked him in the eye, and lowered my voice. "I can relieve my own damn tension. Unless you have anything to tell me, I'm gonna need you to leave me alone 'cos I've got things to do."

His smirk returned but he was smart enough to remove it before I slapped it off his face. "Come on, Darcy. I know you don't completely trust me, okay? But you were the one who sought me out, and now you need me."

I clenched my jaw. "I don't *need* anyone."

Don't want *to need anyone.*

"Sure you don't." He nodded condescendingly. "Okay, we'll play it your way. You don't need me. Fine. But right now, I'm hungry and you must be too. You've been on your feet all day, so why don't you let me take you for dinner and you can keep pretending you hate me if that makes you happy."

I did hate him. In that moment, I hated the way he'd marched into my workplace without warning and told me what I was doing next. I hated that he found me so damn easy to read, and mostly I hated that the way he'd whispered in my ear had made my panties wet.

"Why? Why do you want to take me out for dinner?" I asked, trying to take my focus away from thoughts of his lips all over my body. "And now I think of it, how did you even know I was here today? What were you doing? Circling this place to see if I was at work?"

I knew he'd checked up on me before we 'met,' but there was no way he could have known my work schedule; it changed every week.

"Paranoia will drive you crazy." He put his hand on my shoulders and turned me around, gently ushering me outside so we were no longer lingering in the doorway. "I finished work an hour ago. I swung by your apartment. I called you but your phone was off, so I tried coming here. You're not so hard to track down."

In the busy street, I knew I couldn't reach up and strangle him for being such an arrogant prick. *Unfortunately.* "You still haven't told me why you were so desperate to reach me."

"Never accuse a guy of being desperate." His hands remained firmly on my shoulders. "Here's what I'm thinking. You think you know who I am. You're wrong. And if you're so wrong about that, I can't allow you to play detective alone because, if I let you, you're gonna get yourself killed. My job ain't a joke, princess. You're messing with things you don't understand. So, I'm taking you out to eat right now so you can start learning to trust me and leave all of this in my hands. Understand?"

"Don't patronize me, shit head," I snarled. "And don't underestimate me."

He grabbed hold of my arm, looking up and down the street as if to check we weren't being watched. Dumb move in downtown Chicago. Someone's always watching. "Don't force me to be an asshole. Get in the fucking car."

The grit in his voice was another direct hit at my core, and although I was still glowering at him, I let him drag me to his car and throw me in the passenger seat. When he climbed into the driver's side, I stared straight ahead, rage bubbling within me. I felt sure if I'd looked at him, I'd have landed a sharp hook on his chiseled jaw.

I had no idea where we were going, and I sure as hell wasn't going to ask. I'd felt stressed before I left work, but now I was furious. With myself for being such a shitty sleuth and getting my cover blown so fast, and with Drake for coming to my workplace and trying to tell me what I could and couldn't do. Just because I didn't have a plan yet, it didn't mean I wasn't going to figure one out. I had no choice but to think of something because every day, hour, minute… every second Matteo was in jail, I was failing him the way the system failed him. The way everyone else had failed him. Me letting him down just wasn't an option.

Angry tears burned the backs of my eyes and I stared ahead, silently screaming at them to go away. I didn't need Drake thinking he'd upset me. My tears weren't a symbol of weakness and I refused to allow him even a moment to think of me as some pathetic, weepy girl who couldn't control her emotions. That wasn't me. I kept that shit for when I was alone.

"Darcy."

His voice was softer now, and I knew he'd seen the moisture forming a fine sheen over my eyes, blurring my vision. Instead of answering, I kept inwardly willing the tears away, not shifting my gaze from the now distorted road ahead. When I didn't answer him, he gave up and didn't say another word until we stopped in the parking lot of a White Castle just on the edge of the city.

He seems to know a lot of places just on the outskirts of the city. Shady fucker.

"White Castle? Really?" I slammed the door shut and stood looking at him over the roof of his car.

He raised an eyebrow. "I'm sorry. I didn't know you expected a fancy dinner. In case you didn't notice, you're not exactly dressed for a fine dining experience."

I glanced down at my work uniform; a short black skirt and a tight-fitting red t-shirt. I knew perfectly well that my hair was its usual end-of-the-day disheveled mess and falling free from the hair tie that was supposed to hold it back. "Well, you're overdressed for this place, and in case you'd forgotten, you didn't ask to bring me here, you burst into my workplace and dragged me into your car. You may as well have clubbed me over the head like the caveman you clearly are."

Instead of engaging in my tantrum, Finn walked around the car and stood in front of me. "Darcy Ryan, will you please have dinner with me?"

Chapter 8
Finn

This woman was going to be the death of me. Literally if I didn't get my shit together.

I couldn't say what possessed me to go find her once my shift was over, but something in me needed to keep her out of trouble, and the only way I had a shot at doing that was by convincing her I wasn't the person she thought I was. No matter what she said, I knew I'd gained a little of her trust. If I hadn't, she'd have run. Darcy Ryan was good at running. She'd run from a lot of places in her twenty-five years. Not that I blamed her. I would never let on that I knew her background. I needed her to tell me herself because then I'd know for sure that she believed I was on her side. Best I could tell, Torres was the only person she really trusted and he was no good to her behind bars. She was gonna need someone on the outside, something more substantial than the superficial friendships she'd formed at work.

After ordering–a Bacon Cheese Slider and fries for her, and a Chicken Ring Slider and fries for me–we sat opposite each other at a table by the window. Darcy had calmed some since taking her seat, but she refused to look at me, instead focusing outside at the cars driving in and out of the parking lot.

"Ask me anything," I said, laying my hands flat on the table in front of me, palms up. "Anything you want."

"You got anything new for me?" she asked, without turning her head.

"Not yet. Working on it."

"Then I have no other questions."

I stared at her as she continued to ignore me. Wisps of her dark hair had escaped from her ponytail, and her pretty blue eyes were tinged with sadness. Or maybe tiredness.

"Okay." I sighed. "I'll talk. I'm thirty-one years old. Lived in Chicago all my life. My family life was a fucking disaster when I was growing up, and I–"

She looked at me sharply, her eyes now alight with anger. "Do I look like I want to know your life story? The only thing I want from you is answers about Matteo's case and something that will prove his innocence. I don't need to know anything else. I prefer not to."

"Why?" I challenged, leaning toward her slightly. "What are you afraid of?"

"I'm not afraid of anything. I just don't want or need to know about your life. You're a cop. I made a foolish move by trying to find out what you know, and maybe you'll help me or maybe you won't. Either way, once this is over, I'm not anticipating seeing you again, so let's just bury this getting to know you exercise right now and stick to the facts."

"The facts? The facts are that you have less than no idea what you're gonna do if I can't find the answers you want, and any other option available to you will end with you in a body bag. And for what? Torres will still be in jail and you'll be dead." I watched as her focus dropped to the table. "Darcy, this isn't going to be over in a week and you know it. And you might not want to admit it but, right now, I am the best hope you have of getting Torres out. You cannot possibly do this alone. So, you wanna just save us another argument and admit that you need my help?"

I didn't take my gaze away from her. I could see her battling internally over whether or not she wanted to throw her juice in my face. Eventually, she looked up at me. "Okay. I need your help."

"Do you trust me?"

Darcy reached for her glass, spinning it around slowly between her hands, her stare fixed on it like she was trying to hypnotize herself or something. "I don't trust anyone. So when I tell you I don't trust you, it's nothing personal."

"Yet you're still willing to ask for my help?"

Her head snapped up to look at me again. "Is this some kind of psychological assessment? I got issues, okay? I won't allow myself to put all my faith in you because the truth is, you're probably going to fuck me over. Maybe not right away, but eventually. I trust you as much as I can and that's scary as shit to me. Don't push me."

For maybe the second time in my whole life, my heart did some weird thing in my chest. I knew this woman was gonna get under my skin; she was passionate and fiery and sexy as hell. But that glimpse into her vulnerable side affected me more than I was ready to admit.

She ain't the only one with issues.

Our food arrived, and instead of focusing on the unwelcome sensation in my chest, I focused on eating. The atmosphere around us had shifted. Darcy had stopped throwing death glares my way and the badass woman I'd found at the coffee shop had been replaced by... I don't know... maybe the real Darcy. The scared little girl I knew was underneath her bravado. It wouldn't have taken a degree in psychology to figure her out. It was part of my job to quickly locate a person's weaknesses and break them down. That was how I got confessions. But I never expected her to crumble so fast and I felt like an asshole for stripping her of her spirit. That wasn't what I wanted. I just wanted her to swear she'd calm her ass down and let me handle the dangerous stuff.

"Why are you doing this, Drake?"

Her voice was barely a whisper, and I looked up to find her staring at me. "What do you mean?" I asked, buying myself some time.

"Why are you helping me?"

I threw a fry into my mouth and chewed it slowly, wiping my hands on a napkin as I contemplated my answer. The whole time, her gaze didn't falter.

"You mean, aside from the fact that you barreled into this whole thing?" She nodded and I continued with a sigh. "There are a lot of reasons. I don't know you, so it really shouldn't matter to me whether you get yourself killed or not, but in spite of what you think, I'm not the kind of guy who could let that happen. Your intentions with me weren't exactly genuine, but the reason you came to me was. Whatever way you saw this going down, you needed me to get Torres out of jail. I don't believe he belongs there, and I think there's some corrupt bullshit happening inside my department. So… I'm helping you because I wanna ensure the real killer gets put away. And I'm helping *you* because…" I paused, throwing my head back for a second before looking at her again. "Because you're not the total pain in the ass I thought you were when I first met you."

What? It was the best I could do without saying she was the only person I'd gotten even close to caring about in a long damn time. Besides, Darcy Ryan was not a hearts and flowers kind of girl. Best I could tell, she had little interest in over-the-top cliché words or gestures.

The corner of her mouth quirked into a half smile. "Well, that's high praise."

I smirked at her. "Suck it up, buttercup. I'm not so good at compliments."

"That's not true. The night we met, you said I'm a different kind of pretty. That was a good compliment." She spoke with a hint of teasing in her voice.

"I'm not good at forced, over-thought compliments," I corrected myself, then leaned in a little closer to her. "But when it comes to genuine, in the moment compliments… I'm your man."

In spite of herself, she laughed, shaking her head.

"What do you say we get out of here?" I suggested. "I'll take you home and you can go take that hot bubble bath you were talking about before."

Chapter 9
Darcy

From the second I saw Finn standing in the coffee shop, arrogant grin fixed firmly on his face, I'd wanted to get as far away from him as possible. Too bad he practically kidnapped me and dragged me to White Castle, which, in spite of my protests, was pretty damn good.

Since he had no new information for me, I didn't want to be around him, but somewhere between him throwing me into his car after work and arriving at my apartment after eating, something changed. I wasn't stupid enough to not know that he'd chosen every word he'd spoken carefully to get the info he wanted or needed from me. I let him know only as much as I was comfortable with, but I also knew I *could* trust him. Sure, my instincts had been way off when I started this whole thing, but the persona he'd shown in the courtroom was not who he really was. That was his cover–the person he showed to the outside world.

As much as it pained me, I suspected he and I were alike in a lot of ways.

The last time Finn had been in my apartment, we'd made out against my front door then had a fight which left me angry, confused, and in serious need of some relief from the build-up of tension. As I watched him standing by my door, I had a flashback of him pinning my arms above my head and kissing me. I bit my lip and quickly turned away so he couldn't tell what I was thinking.

"I'll make some coffee," I told him, heading for the kitchen. "Take a seat."

When I returned with our drinks, I sat beside him on the couch, placing the steaming mugs on the coffee table in front of us.

"This is a nice place," Finn said, leaning back as he looked around the room.

"You don't need to be polite. I mean, the apartment's fine but it's nothing special."

It was the best I could afford, and it *was* fine. A small, simple, one bedroom apartment that was ideal for me. Safe enough and close to work; I really didn't require anything more.

"It's more homely than my place."

I smirked at him. "Well, you're a man. I imagine you're a fan of minimalism. Maybe the occasional stereotypical guy movie poster here and there, and I bet the only thing in your fridge is beer."

Finn threw me a look of mock horror, his jaw dropping. "You underestimate me, Miss Ryan. I also have frozen pizza, and some dirty magazines under my bed."

"How retro of you. You should consider streaming some porn through your phone like a real man."

He laughed out loud and I couldn't help smiling. Finn's genuine smile was something I hadn't seen much of, which was a shame. When he smiled, there was no longer any sign of the arrogant dude who'd been at the coffee house earlier. His eyes sparkled, and not with the twisted joy he got from annoying me. The first night I'd met him, and most times I'd seen him, he seemed to carry tension with him. He had a constant air of seriousness. Seeing him lighten up was another strong indication that there was way more to him than I thought.

And I most definitely miscalculated when I thought he wasn't my type.

He was clean shaven and smartly dressed; he kinda looked like a model, the kind you'd see on billboards modeling Ralph Lauren clothing. He *wasn't* my usual type. I usually liked my guys bigger built, and I favored dark hair over Drake's blond, but he was an incredible-looking guy.

Besides, it wasn't really about that.

"You have a lot of photos of you and the Torres'," Finn said, his smile fading. I followed his gaze to the photo he was looking at. It was the one I'd looked at the first night I'd officially met him. The one of the three of us at Matteo and Rebecca's wedding.

"Yeah." I sighed. "Like I said before, Matteo's my best friend. We were all friends."

"Can I ask you something?" I shrugged a shoulder and nodded. "Did Rebecca ever have a problem with you and Matteo being friends?"

Laughing, I said, "No more than any other girl would when she found out the guy she liked had a female best friend. She asked all the usual questions about whether we were secretly into each other, and if we'd ever hooked up. When she got the answers, she was okay with it. I felt like…" I paused, unsure whether to reveal this piece of information. It said more about me than I'd usually admit, but since he seemed to know plenty about me already, concealing it wouldn't have made a lot of difference. "I felt like she thought I wasn't a threat because she was prettier than me."

Rebecca truly was stunning. The kind of woman who turned heads every time she left the house. She oozed sex appeal and she knew it. I had no issue with my own looks, but I always felt as though she thought she was the better looking out of the two of us, and I really didn't care about that. I'd never been a competitive person and, even though she'd probably have been able to make Matty ditch me from his life if she'd wanted to, I was never jealous of her. Fact was, if he'd wanted to go, he'd have gone whether I was jealous or not, so I chose not. I always expected people to leave, so what was the point in adding to the hurt I'd feel eventually by worrying about it before it happened? As it turned out, my attitude toward her worked in my favor. She knew I didn't want Matty the way she did and then she grew to like me.

Or I thought she did. That was up for debate now since I didn't think I'd ever really known her at all.

"Bullshit," Finn said, disrupting my thoughts.

I raised a skeptical eyebrow. "Oh, you didn't think she was hot?"

"On the surface, sure. Not gonna lie and say I never checked out her ass as she walked by. But beside you? Uh-uh. In my opinion, Matteo made a shitty choice picking her over you."

"There was never a choice. He and I met because we were in the same classes. I sat at the back, scowling at anyone who looked at me for too long, and he was the only person brave enough to talk to me." I chuckled. "He was persistent. Like the stray cat that follows you home. At first, you tell it to go away because you don't want a damn cat. You're happy on your own. But it lurks by your front door, meowing, looking up at you because it wants you to pet it. After a while, you give in and start to love it. That was our friendship. I never really understood why he tried so hard with me. It was years before I was brave enough to ask."

Revealing that would be way too much information.

"So, you two really are just friends? There's nothing between you at all?"

"No." I laughed. "There was this one time, back when we first started hanging out. We got totally trashed at a party. I don't even remember who started it or why, but we kissed for a little while, and I felt nothing. We stopped it pretty quickly, and afterward, we laughed about how silly it was because while we love each other very much, there was never a spark." I shook my head. "I wish I could explain it better. When I look at Matteo, I see a friend. That's it."

Surprising me, Finn changed the course of the conversation. "Is that why you're trying so hard for him now? I mean, sounds like he really fought for you. For your friendship."

I'd never looked at it from that perspective before. But in a weird way, he was kind of right. Matteo was the only person who'd really wanted a place in my life without wanting anything from me.

"Maybe," I said. "Maybe that is a part of it." But it was also the injustice of the whole thing. Matteo was *not* a murderer. Was I supposed to just let that slide and accept the jury's stupid decision? "Matty was–and this is going to sound real pathetic but– he was my first ever real friend." Finn stared at me, sadness creeping into his blue eyes and I held up my hand. "Don't you dare pity me, Drake."

"Pity you? I don't pity you, Darcy. You don't need or deserve it because you're not a victim. Rebecca Torres… she played the part of the tough girl, but it seems to me all she ever wanted was attention. Look where it got her. But you?" He shook his head. "You don't need anyone's pity. Least of all mine."

I stared at him for a moment, unable to understand how I'd got him so wrong. *You got him wrong because the way you saw him is how he wants to be seen. How about that, huh?*

In the moment of silence, I picked up my cup of coffee that I'd almost forgotten about and took a sip before placing it back down and looking right into Finn's eyes. "How much do you know about me, Drake?"

He didn't show any signs of regret for snooping into my past. I can't say how I knew he had, it was just a feeling.

"More than I should," he admitted, without looking away from me. "But probably not nearly as much as there is to know."

I nodded slowly then swallowed before speaking. "Can you be more specific?" The fact that he didn't break eye contact told me he wasn't going to lie to me. This was so different to the first time he'd been to my apartment. Then, even when he'd looked right at me, his eyes had shielded his true intentions. Now, his eyes were clear. Open. Honest.

"I can," he said. "But I didn't tell you I knew anything because I wanted you to feel comfortable enough to tell me yourself."

"I've known you for five minutes. *If* I were to tell someone about my life, it would usually be after much longer. It took Matteo ten months to get it out of me. That doesn't include the couple of months prior when he was still trying to break down my barriers."

"So don't tell me. But, Darcy, I want you to know that anything I know… I didn't dig around so I could be an asshole. I did it because, like you, I need to know who I'm dealing with. I didn't think I'd find anything."

He continued to look into my eyes, and with every second that passed, the intensity in the room grew stronger. I kinda hated that he knew my past. Kinda liked that I didn't have to tell him. Kinda scared myself because I had the strangest feeling that, at some point, I *would* have told him.

"My family life sucked," I said, slowly sinking back into the couch. "One of the things you might have found was that I didn't spend a whole lot of time with my parents. They were volatile. Both of them. I grew up thinking it was normal to be woken up in the middle of the night by the sound of screaming and shattering glass, or loud thuds – usually the sound of my mother being thrown against something, or my mom managing to throw my dad to the ground when he was drunk enough to be too weak to stay upright. I thought all kids got yelled at all the time. I was placed with other families a lot. I was lucky because most of the families were nice to me. The first time I was taken away, I think I was six years old. The people I lived with were so kind. I didn't want to go home, and when they let me go back to my parents, I realized. Nobody wanted to keep me." Without warning, I saw myself back in my room at my parents' house, sitting on my bed harboring a feeling I didn't understand. Tension because I was waiting for the screaming to start again. And this overwhelming sadness because I'd felt loved and loved people in return, and they'd sent me back to my home full of pain and anger. In the pit of my stomach, I felt the physical sensation of fear, as if I'd never left that room or that house.

I risked a quick look up at Drake, but he didn't speak. He just waited for me to continue.

"After that, anytime I was placed with a new family, I wasn't nice to them. Didn't trust them. What was the point in liking them? Whether it was days, weeks, or months, eventually they'd make me go home."

"Did you miss your parents when you weren't with them?" Finn asked, his voice steady. He was being super careful not to let me hear any hint of him feeling sorry for me. He didn't need to try to hide it though. I could kinda feel it from him. But it wasn't pity. More like… understanding.

"At first. Even though I hated how much noise they always made, the first time I was away from them, I wanted to go home. I missed my mom especially. Out of the two of them, she treated me better than my dad. But after a while, I stopped missing them. I didn't want to go back to them. I wanted the peace and kindness I got from the people I didn't know. Eventually, I started running away. I was probably about ten the first time. I was living with good people, but once the whispers started that it was time for me to go home soon, I decided I wasn't going back. So I packed up as much as I could stuff into a backpack and snuck out in the middle of the night. The cops found me pretty easily because I didn't know where or how to hide. They picked me up at the bus station. I ran away a bunch of times after that. As I got older, it got easier. I managed to get away for longer. One time I was missing for a month." I paused and shook my head at the memory. "It's bad, isn't it?" I asked, looking up at him. "I was starving, scared, and cold for four weeks. Dirty from having nowhere to shower, and barely any clothes to change into. I slept on park benches, in shop doorways. But that felt better to me than going home."

Finn lifted his hand as if to reach for me, but dropped it before touching me. "Your mom died, right?"

I nodded. "When I was sixteen. The cause of death was officially ruled as an accidental overdose. I'm not so sure it was an accident. I think she'd had enough. Shortly after, I was taken away from my dad permanently because of his drinking and violence. Without my mom, I was the only person he had to fight with, and after he almost killed me, he went to jail and I was officially parentless." This time, Finn did reach for my hand, but I moved it away. "Please. Just… don't."

I felt vulnerable enough after revealing my past. Allowing myself to show any sign of vulnerability was unacceptable to me. Finn hadn't even heard all of my story; the darker parts of what had happened to me were firmly locked away. But the way Finn looked at me told me he knew those parts too. He knew my dad had beaten me almost daily after my mom died. He'd broken my jaw, cracked my ribs, blackened my eyes, and so much more. The day I almost died at his hands, he'd been in the process of strangling me when the cops burst in after the neighbors alerted them to my screams.

But I didn't want to be viewed as a victim. In fact, nothing angered me more, because I'd risen above it. Above all of it. The only thing I was grateful to my parents for was the fact that my mom – in spite of her issues – had managed to squirrel away enough money to see me through college. It was the only thing of use she'd ever given me, and it was because of that one thing that I wasn't living on the streets again, begging for spare change. Probably sounds pretty crazy after everything I went through, but I considered myself one of the lucky ones. *I'm alive.* I didn't require anyone's sympathy.

"My life hasn't been so different to yours, Darcy," Finn said. "Except my parents were junkies and now they're both dead. And I could tell you more about that, and I will if you want to hear it. But right now… maybe that's enough heavy stuff for today."

"Yeah. Enough. But if you do want to talk about it sometime, we can."

Finn gave me a nod, then, after looking at me for a few moments, he said, "I should go soon. I've probably taken enough of your time today, huh?"

His words caused an odd pang in my stomach. *This is why you don't allow yourself to be vulnerable. It messes with your head.* Telling him about my life was a huge and potentially dangerous thing to do. Not dangerous because of what he might do with the information; he already knew it anyway. But it was dangerous for me to allow him a glimpse of the real me. Of where I came from. It was one thing for him to know about my past, but me willingly sharing it was something else.

I forced my focus back on him and away from my messed up thoughts. "Right. I recall you telling me to take a bath. The smell must be out of control by now."

He smiled. "You smell great. Like coffee and junk food. Two of my favorite things."

I narrowed my eyes on him but I couldn't help giving in to a laugh. "I think the smell of coffee is never going to leave me now. I've been working at the coffee shop for so long,

66

it's permanently embedded itself into me. But the junk food smell needs to go. I'm thinking strawberry scented bath bubbles, and maybe vanilla scented candles."

Finn placed his coffee cup on the table then stood up. "I definitely need to go. With that thought in my head, I won't be needing to look at magazines or stream anything through my phone."

I stood too. "Pervert."

He smiled at me again, his blue eyes meeting mine, then he shook his head and turned to walk toward the door. I started to follow him to see him out but he stopped abruptly, turning to me and causing me to walk right into him. To stop me stumbling, he gripped my hips, holding me while I regained my balance, my hands resting on the tops of his arms to steady myself. Slowly, I looked up at him, my eyes moving from his chest to his face, my heart suddenly beating hard.

Without a word, he moved one hand from my hip to gently stroke my cheek, pushing a strand of my hair away from my face. His gaze never faltered as he leaned in, softly brushing his lips against mine. War raged between my mind and my body. My limbs were slowly weakening, and I wanted to keep on kissing him because, damn, it felt good. But my mind? It screamed at me to make him leave. While the two things battled against each other, I parted my lips slightly as his tongue lightly pressed against them, seeking entry.

Too much, Darcy. This is too much. He's getting too close.

Digging deep inside myself, I gently pushed him back. "I can't do this."

Finn refused to let go of me, one hand still on my hip, the other resting on the back of my neck. His touch was so gentle but that only made it worse. If he'd kissed me the way he had the first time and slammed me against the wall, I might have been able to handle it, but this was too gentle.

Way too caring.

"Why not?" he asked, his voice low and soft against my ear, making shivers ripple through me as his breath caressed my skin.

I closed my eyes, trying to block out everything I wanted right then. "I can't… you…" I paused to catch my breath and swallowed hard. "You can't care about me, Drake."

"Who says I do?" His mouth hovered by my neck, and when I didn't answer, his lips found the sensitive skin there, weakening my already pathetic resolve. Because I *did* want him. And I wanted him to care.

And that's exactly why you have to make it stop.

His lips softly trailed along my jawline, making my whole body tremble.

"Drake," I murmured, my eyes closing again. "Please. Don't."

"Don't what?" He pulled me in closer.

I gathered up my strength and pushed him back with a little more force, and as he stepped back, God, I missed the contact. I wanted to touch him, but if I let him near me… I just couldn't do it.

"Don't screw with me. You need to go now." He took a step toward me as if to reach out for me again but I held my hands up and shook my head. Unwelcome and unexpected tears pooled in my eyes and I blinked, hoping to make them go away. "Please just go."

His eyes seemed to burn right through me. "I'm not screwing with you, Darcy. I *do* care about you, but if it makes it easier for you, we can pretend I don't."

I shook my head. "I can't do that. I can't let you get any closer. You already know more about me than almost anyone else in the world. This isn't…" Again, I had to stop and take a deep breath. My mind and my body were still at odds and I couldn't think straight. Especially not with those damn blue eyes staring at me, trying to read my mind. Trying to delve further than I wanted him to go. "Drake, I just needed your help. That's all."

A flash of what looked like hurt flickered in his eyes, but it was gone before I could tell if I'd imagined it or not. God, he really was a lot like me. But slightly braver. Because there was no way in hell I would admit to even liking him, much less caring about him. My insides began to hurt in a way they'd never hurt before, not even when my own parents were using me as a punch bag; I'd always known what to expect from them. This was different. This was me feeling something for a man; something beyond friendship or even just basic desire. My entire being ached to get closer to him, to let him make me feel and attempt to glue together the pieces of me that had been broken for so long.

Looking up at him again, trying not to let any hint of my feelings show, I said, "I can't get any closer to you, okay? It's too much of a risk."

It hurts, but I can't do it.

"You think it's not a risk for me too?" he snapped. He stepped toward me again and placed his hands on my shoulders, gripping hard. "The only reason you came into my life was to use me for your own fucking gain, so don't talk to me about risk!"

"If that's how you feel then you really need to leave before this gets any more complicated."

"I don't want to leave, okay? For the first time in my goddamn life, I don't want to walk away!"

"What the hell do you think is going to happen here, huh?" I pushed him off again and turned away, pacing. I was struggling to breathe, to think, with him staring at me. "What you said was true." Facing him again, I shrugged, hoping to hell I was fooling him, because I wasn't fooling myself. "I was using you. I *am* using you. Once all this is over, we're not going to skip off into the sunset together. You'll go find some other person to save and I'll go back to doing my own thing."

"Your own thing? What does that even mean? You work in a fucking coffee shop and then hide up here in your apartment!"

The sting of his words was another stark reminder that he needed to get out of my apartment, out of my life, immediately. His words shouldn't have affected me. I'm Darcy freaking Ryan, and nobody got close enough to hurt me. Ever.

"Fuck you, Drake!" I spat. "You don't get to judge me and my life when yours is no better!"

"You're right. My life is as fucked up as yours. We're just two fucked up people with fucked up pasts, trying to figure out how not to fuck up our futures. But, you know what? If you keep on pretending not to care about anything, some day, you really won't."

Moisture burned behind my eyes because he wasn't being fair. "Why do you think I'm doing this? You think I put my life at risk because I don't care about anything? I care about my best friend being screwed over by someone. By someone *you* know! I care that some murdering asshole is walking around without a care in the goddamn world, knowing what he did. Knowing someone else is serving his sentence! I care about the fact that I might not be able to fix this!" The tears finally spilled over, the anger and panic and outright fear overwhelming me, leaving me in body-shaking sobs.

Finn grabbed me and pulled me close to him, but once again, I shoved him away.

I don't need him. Don't want to need him. Won't need him.

When he reached for me a second time, I balled my hands into fists and pummeled his chest. For a moment, he let me, but when I showed no signs of giving up, he grabbed hold of my wrists.

"Stop!" he yelled. "Just stop!"

I glared at him for a second, tears still streaming down my face.

Those. Freaking. Eyes. I don't know what the hell kind of voodoo powers he possessed, but with every second he stared at me, my anger ebbed away a little more. When he was certain I wasn't going to punch him again, he let go of my wrists and placed his hands either side of my face.

He crushed his lips against my mouth and I was done fighting him. I wound my arms around his neck and let him move me back toward the couch, slowly pushing me down before climbing on top of me. His lips barely left mine, and I reached for his tie, loosening it before dropping it to the floor. He pushed my t-shirt up and over my head, and as the material slipped from his fingers, his gaze moved from my face down to my chest. His eyes flashed with need and I gripped the collar of his shirt and pulled him closer. He watched me as I deftly unbuttoned it then slipped my hands inside the material and slid it over his shoulders. As he shrugged it off, I glanced down at his lean, but perfectly toned chest.

How did you ever think he wasn't your type? Oh, right. He's a bent cop.

That fear was still heavily engrained in my mind, but I knew him now. Or at least, I thought I knew him. Sensing my hesitation, Finn lightly kissed me.

"Stop thinking," he whispered against my mouth. "If you want me to leave, then I'll leave. I'll do what you asked of me and I'll stay out of your way until I have information for you. But that's not what either of us wants."

That's not what I want. I want you to stay.

As he brushed the hair from my eyes, I reached for his hand, linking my fingers through his, fighting against every deep-rooted instinct telling me to let him go. "This is by far the dumbest thing I've ever done."

"Dumber than trying to screw me for information?"

I nodded. "Way dumber."

I stared deep into his eyes, searching for any sign in those sparkling blues that he was a liar. That he was messing with me. I came up empty.

"But, Darcy, if you'd been right about me, you could have ended up dead."

I shrugged. "When you're dead, you can't feel pain." Something changed in his eyes when I said those words and the air around us suddenly felt thicker, heavier. I didn't need to tell him that the only real reason for me to keep going, to keep on living, was because I wouldn't see Matteo ending his days in jail. My life without my best friend was everything Finn said. It was lonely and virtually meaningless.

There was only one person in the world who would notice I was even gone.

Finn's stare was intense as I fought to keep my thoughts from overwhelming me. "I'm not gonna hurt you, okay?"

I believed him. I believed him as much as my battered, screwed up heart could. But as much as I believed it, and as good as it felt to have someone touch me so gently, I couldn't handle it. I wanted, *needed*, the guy who'd kissed me hard and pinned me against the door. That guy didn't have feelings for me and I didn't have feelings for him. Those two people didn't care about each other, and I needed to fool myself for a little longer that those people still existed.

I shuffled slightly, lifting my back from the couch to unclip my own bra, and discarded it with my top and Finn's shirt. Again, his eyes flashed and I wriggled out from underneath him and stood up. "Come with me."

I headed for the bathroom and I could feel Finn's eyes on me as he followed. I reached into the shower to turn it on. As steam began to fill the room, I pulled him to me, raking my fingers through his hair as I moved my mouth over his.

It didn't take long to shed the rest of our clothes, and Finn pushed me into the cubicle, my back hitting the cold tiles with force. As the hot water rained down on us, I looked up at him, my chest heaving, and he lowered his head and took my nipple into his mouth as his hands dug into my hips. This was what I needed. His teeth grazing against my hardened nipples as his hands moved roughly against my skin. I didn't need the foreplay, I needed him inside me, and I pressed my hips against his to show my frustration. He moved a hand in between us, his fingers reaching between my legs for the sensitive bundle of nerves that was throbbing for his touch. He pushed his fingers against it, sending a bolt of electricity through my body.

"Drake," I moaned, grinding against his fingers. "Please."

Before I had a chance to draw breath, he'd grabbed my wrists and held them above my head—just like before—his grip so tight I had no chance of breaking free. My heart pounded harder.

"Don't think I don't know what you're doing, Darcy." His tone was low, commanding, and I couldn't take my eyes off his lips, which were so close to mine I could almost taste him. "Right now, I'll let you have your way, but you don't get to fight this next time. Next time, I call the shots."

"What makes you think there'll be a next time?" I tilted my head slightly, challenging him, and he tightened his grip a little more. Steam swirled around us as the water continued to pour down over us. I watched the droplets fall from his face onto his chest, each one trickling a path down to his stomach.

"Call it intuition." His words forced me to look up at him again, and as I did, I saw just how serious he was. He wasn't in this for one night only, and as much as I wanted to run from that, from my own feelings, I knew he wouldn't let me.

Words I never thought I'd say to him, or to anyone, tumbled from my lips. "You win."

He smirked then dropped my hands. I wound my arms around his neck as he lifted me up, my legs wrapping around his waist.

Finn gave me no time to speak or think; he slammed inside me and I closed my eyes, my breath leaving me in sharp bursts with every thrust. I clung to him as I got lost in the rhythm of our bodies rocking against each other, the intensity building higher and higher until we both cried out, our skin soaked in sweat and streaming water.

Chapter 10
Finn

Holy. Shit.

My gaze flicked around the now familiar bedroom I'd woken up in, taking in the vivid red walls and sleek black modern furniture. She had a cool as hell dresser with one of those mirrors with lightbulbs around it, and in between the badass furnishings were small signs that she wasn't the ice queen she pretended to be. A small teddy bear was perched on the dresser by the mirror, and there were some postcards on the walls in frames that showed a selection of life quotes, like those corny motivational pictures that fly around on social media.

The clock on the wall told me it was almost seven, and the empty space beside me told me that Darcy was probably not going to make this morning easy.

I had an hour and thirty minutes before I had to be in the office, so I laid back and closed my eyes, thinking about how I'd ended up in Darcy's bed.

I'd known from the start I'd end up there. And not just because she'd set out to screw me. She was everything a fuck-up like me liked in a woman. Beautiful, tough, loyal, and sweet as hell underneath it all. The only reason I could see through her bullshit was because I was the same way.

I flinched at the memory of some of the things I'd said to her the night before. I'd let my guard down too soon, but damn, the woman was messing with my head. One part of me wanted to protect her, the other wanted to fuck her until she couldn't walk. It'd been a long-ass time since I'd wanted to do both of those things to the same girl. Sure, she drove me fucking crazy around eighty percent of the time, but for the other twenty percent she showed me who she really was?

It was worth every goddamn second.

My dick stirred to life as I pictured her naked body in front of me, on top of me, underneath me. I made her keep her word after I fucked her in the shower the way she wanted. Whatever we had might not have meant much, but hell, it was the most I'd felt in years. So, we slowed things down. I got to enjoy every fucking perfect curve of her body. I got to experience something that–at a guess–very few men had experienced before. Don't get me wrong, there was nothing virginal about Darcy Ryan. She knew what she wanted and she wasn't shy, but she wasn't the kind of girl who gave it up easily. Not even for a release. Truth was, she would have had no issue fucking me just for information because she needed it and I didn't mean a thing to her. When she first met me, it would have been an act of desperation and nothing more. Now? I wasn't a stranger anymore. This was new territory for her, best I could tell.

But what happened now?

I stretched my arms out over my head then climbed out of the bed, heading to the bathroom to find some of my clothes. My underwear and pants were still on the bathroom floor, and I pulled them on and walked through to the kitchen. Darcy sat at the kitchen table, her dark hair twisted on top of her head in a messy bun, her face free of make-up, and she wore an oversized t-shirt. Her hands were wrapped around a mug of coffee as she stared into space.

She looked hot the night I met her. She looked sexy as hell in her work uniform. But sitting there, totally natural… she was beautiful.

"Morning," I said, standing in the doorway and leaning against the doorframe.

Her head snapped toward me and her eyes traveled over my chest before resting on my face. "Hey."

I nodded in the direction of her coffee. "Mind if I get some of that?"

"Help yourself."

Darcy didn't move as I entered the kitchen and poured some coffee into the mug that, presumably, she'd left there for me. There were no others lying around, and I smiled to myself that she'd done that. With my drink made, I turned around to face her and rested my back against the counter. "Are you okay?"

She glanced up at me from beneath her long lashes and gave a single nod. "Yeah. I'm okay."

This was the real bitch of not really knowing her. Sure, I could see through her a lot of the time, but this was a little different. This was Darcy after letting her barriers down, and I felt like she wasn't sure whether to keep them down or put the walls back up. Or maybe I was wrong and they were already back in place.

"You're gonna have to stop staring at me," she said. She wasn't looking at me anymore, she was looking ahead at the wall, and I still couldn't read anything from her expression or tone.

"Do I *have* to?"

She flicked her eyes in my direction for a second, then back to the white wall in front of her. "What do you want from me? Huh?"

If she thought I was having this conversation with the side of her head, she was mistaken. I didn't speak until she finally turned to look at me. Her eyes were heavy with questions. I pushed away from the counter and sat down beside her, placing my mug on the table. Again, her gaze dropped down to my chest and I found it impossible to stop a smug grin from spreading across my face.

"Quit it, Drake." But she bit her lip, and I could see her lightening up, still smiling a little. I placed my hand on her cheek and she closed her eyes and leaned into it for a second before pulling away and sitting up straighter. "What are we doing?"

"Right now?" I leaned back in my chair and took a sip of my coffee. "Right now, we're having breakfast." I glanced down at my mug. "For me, coffee is breakfast."

She shook her head. "You know what I mean."

As I lifted my head to look at her, I said, "Looking ahead isn't part of the deal here, sweetheart. I haven't forgotten why you started all this. I'm going to do everything I can to get Torres out of jail, but can't we just keep on getting to know each other too, without worrying about where it'll go?" I paused and ran a hand through my hair. "Just talking about this feels weird when all I really want to do is kiss you."

I was out of my depth with this conversation because I wasn't expecting to feel anything at all, and I wasn't used to having to figure out my feelings because I hadn't had any in a really long time.

I sensed her hesitation, and when she opened her mouth to speak, I interrupted her. "I ain't trying to marry you, lady. I've been there, done that, and I'm not in a rush to—"

"You were married?" she cut in.

Crap. I hadn't intended to blurt that out. Around her, for some reason, I was incapable of doing anything other than telling the truth.

I nodded. "I was. Turns out being married to a cop ain't much fun."

"What happened?"

"I spent more time at work than at home, and she… well, I guess she decided she deserved better. Left me for some guy who works in an office. Regular nine to five guy who'll be home on the weekends and not out on the streets busting bad guys."

"I'm sorry."

"Don't be. Truth is, I should never have married her. If I'd loved her half as much as I should have, maybe I wouldn't have wanted to be at the office so much."

I was the exact opposite of Darcy when I was her age. Younger even. While she put walls up to keep people out, I'd wanted the family I'd been cheated of when I was a kid. When I was twenty-one, I met a woman and decided she would be the one. I liked her. Maybe even loved her. But I never felt even a fraction of the spark I felt with Darcy. Nicki was safe. She was kind, and sweet, and the perfect woman to settle down with.

I just wasn't as ready to settle down as I thought.

"How long were you married?" Darcy asked.

"Four years. I was with her for seven. We've been apart for three years, and I've been officially divorced for a year."

She nodded slowly, and it seemed like my revelation made her see me differently. Something changed in her eyes, like she was seeing me as more than just a cop. More than some guy who was trying to get in her pants… again.

"I'm real easy to get to know, Darcy. All you have to do is ask and I'll tell you anything you want to know."

"I don't…" she trailed off and sighed. "I don't wanna ask questions. I just wanna… can we just do what you said? We'll not look ahead. We'll do what we were supposed to do and get Matteo home where he belongs. And if you want to drop by my work place, or come over, I promise not to bitch at you."

Again, I let out a small laugh. The weight of what she'd said wasn't lost on me. For most, those words wouldn't have been a big deal, but for her? This was a huge step. She didn't want to push me away anymore. She was willing to see how this played out.

"Hey." Her voice snapped me from my thoughts and I looked up at her. "Before you said you wanted to kiss me." She smiled and raised an eyebrow, silently inviting me.

I rested my hand on her cheek again, leaning in just a little closer to her. "Yeah. I did say that."

"So…?"

I didn't need to be asked twice. I took her lower lip into my mouth and gently sucked it before releasing it and kissing her until she moaned into my mouth. She ran a hand slowly down my chest while the other rested on the back of my neck, keeping me close.

"Miss Ryan, you are making me crazy." I closed my eyes and rested my forehead against hers. "I have to go to work."

"You sure?"

I loved the look in her eyes. She wasn't looking at me all doe-eyed like some women did after spending the night with me. And she wasn't looking at me with suspicion anymore. The only thing I could see was desire, like she really had decided to just relax and see where this crazy train took us.

And, fuck, I wanted her just as much.

"I got bad guys to bust," I said. "I was gonna put in a little overtime later too."

For her. To help her, I was willing to put in overtime. Yeah, I was working on the Torres case anyway, but now it was a priority. That I wanted to do something for someone else was a surprise to me. Not because I was a self-centered asshole – it was literally my job to make sure the right person went to jail, and I'd been part of a huge fuck up where Torres was concerned; I needed to fix that. But doing it for Darcy? Doing it because I cared about her being happy again? That was a totally alien feeling. Had I ever wanted to make my wife happy? Sure. And in spite of what she had said, I *did* try. But with her, it never felt like *this*. With her, things were… comfortable. And comfortable was boring as shit. What's the goddamn point in being secure if you're bored? With Darcy, whatever this was, however long it lasted, I knew it was never going to be dull. Not even for a moment.

"Okay," Darcy said, kissing me once more before leaning back in her chair with a sigh that made me want to swipe everything off the table, movie-style, and bury myself inside her. She paused and took a drink of her coffee. "I'm going to see Matteo this afternoon."

Way to kill the mood.

"Okay. Are you planning to tell him anything about…" I paused, gesturing between us with my finger. "About this?"

She nodded slowly. "I think so. I mean, he's gonna ask. He's gonna want to know if I'm any closer to finding anything out, and he knows that to do that I have to get closer to you. I can't lie to him. He'd see through me if I tried."

I stared at her, the reminder of why she'd gotten involved with me making me question what the hell I was doing with her. What if I was wrong about her? What if she *was* just using me for information? Would it even matter to me if she never saw me again once she got what she needed? Maybe. Maybe not.

Bullshit. It matters.

"I can't promise you anything more than I already have."

Darcy's words made me wonder if I'd been spoken my thoughts aloud, but the way she looked at me told me she hadn't needed me to. *Fuck.*

"I'm getting transparent," I said, standing up and taking my cup over to the sink. After placing it down, I took a breath before turning around to face her again. Her eyes had followed me across the room. "I don't need you to promise me anything, Darcy. All I want from you is honesty."

"Right back at ya, Drake."

**

The big problem with needing to dig around in things that should have been left alone was that there was rarely a moment when I was completely alone to get the job done. My office was mine and mine alone, but people walked in and out, asking questions, needing information, asking me to do stuff, to be somewhere, and often with only a second's notice. I didn't have time to hide anything when I needed to leave in a hurry, so working overtime was the only time I really got some space. If I wanted to figure out what had happened to Rebecca Torres, I was gonna have to put in a lot more hours, but I didn't want to draw any unwanted attention to myself. Not until I knew exactly who and what I was dealing with. Some things I could do from home, but others required me to be in the office where I could access all of the case details.

"Yo, Drake."

My head snapped up to see Al standing beside my desk. Lucky for me, I was working on something totally legit because I hadn't heard him walk in. For a big dude, he was stealthy.

"What's up, Al?"

He had a smirk on his face which was pretty unlike him. Al Miller did not smirk. He was a good cop but, most of the time, he had the expression of someone who was deeply uncomfortable. My eyebrows furrowed.

"You have a good time last night?"

Images of Darcy ran through my head, making me glad I was sitting behind a desk. How the hell would Al have known about that, though?

Keeping a perfectly straight face, I said, "What do you mean?"

He gave a short laugh, casually resting his hand on the edge of my desk. "I saw you. At White Castle. With Matteo Torres' side chick."

My pulse began to race as thoughts crashed through my brain at a frightening speed. On the outside, I still maintained my composure; I was a master at hiding my thoughts from people. I'd had to be to survive my childhood, and it was why I was so good at my job.

"That White Castle's a little out of your way," I said, leaning back in my chair, all the time keeping my eyes on him. If I looked away, he'd suspect something was up. I was pissed at him calling Darcy a "side chick" but I had to let it go in the interests of not giving anything away. Yeah, I still trusted him to a degree, but not enough to let slip anything that might cause his psycho brother to go after her.

"I was out for the day with the wife and kids," Al said. "We stopped off for food on the way home. I was gonna come over and say hey, but…" he trailed off and winked at me.

I rolled my eyes. "It wasn't a date, if that's you're thinking. Seems she's having a little trouble accepting Torres' conviction. You know he argued he was set up. She wanted to talk to someone who was involved in the case to find out if we'd really checked out every avenue."

"Is she stupid?" Al snorted. "His lawyers were claiming *we* set him up! Why would she go to a cop for information if she thought we were in on the whole thing?"

"She knew Rebecca Torres was screwing around," I lied. "She doesn't think we had anything to do with a cover up; she thinks we need to find out more about who Rebecca was seeing." Al's face paled a little; a dead giveaway that his fucking brother had something to do with the murder and Al had probably helped clean up the mess. "She has no idea that Rebecca was involved with so many cops. She just asked me to look into it more. I told her the case is closed. That we did look into other suspects, but once the murder weapon was found with Torres' blood on it, it was game over. Looking elsewhere made no sense, and now it's over." I shrugged casually. "She doesn't want to accept that her best friend killed someone. I get that."

"You think she's gonna be trouble?"

"No. I put her mind at ease. She was pretty upset when she came to me. That's why I took her out. I know it was a risky move, but I'm not a complete douchebag. I just wanted to calm her down, and I couldn't take her back to my place. You know I don't take women back to my place. Way too much hassle."

Again, Al grinned, the worry now gone from his face. "Too bad you didn't hit that. She's hot. Cute ass."

Forcing down the urge to punch him for talking about her that way, I laughed. "Can't argue with that. But I ain't getting mixed up with her no matter how hot she is."

"Good call." Al straightened up. "You wanna grab some lunch?"

I looked at the time on my computer screen. Felt like I'd only left Darcy's place a half hour ago, but I'd been working for four hours already. Blowing out a breath, I nodded. "Yeah, I guess we should."

I turned off my laptop and stood up, hoping to hell Al was done questioning me about Darcy. No matter what, and no matter how much I wanted to see her, now *Al* had seen me with her, we were gonna have to be careful.

The urgency to crack this fucking case had just stepped up another level. I hoped I could keep up.

Chapter 11
Darcy

I'd never been nervous to visit Matteo before. I was nervous the first time I visited him in jail because I hadn't known what to expect, and I still approached the place with apprehension because jail is never a nice place to be. But I always sucked it up because, no matter how much the place creeped me out, I could leave. Matteo was stuck there and he needed all the support he could get. His parents and his sister and brother-in-law visited too, but they lived in Minnesota. They couldn't get to him as often as I could. Rebecca's family–in spite of knowing him for years–believed he had killed her, and they wanted nothing to do with him, and the same went for any friends we knew from college. Since I was pretty vocal about his innocence, those friends didn't want to associate with me anymore either. It was no loss for me. I didn't care for most of them anyway. I hated how quickly people had turned on Matty though. They should have known better.

But I digress.

As I walked into the cold, unwelcoming room after being searched, my head was a mess of things I wanted to say to Matteo. I'd rehearsed my words all morning, and all the way there, but as I approached him where he sat behind that damn window–an extra barrier between us that would make whatever I was about to say that much harder–I couldn't remember anything I'd practiced.

He smiled as he always did when I sat down, and, as *I* always did, I swept my eyes over him, making sure he looked as expected. His curly hair was messy as ever, and he was growing some stubble on his chin. His eyes were still lacking their old sparkle, but all in all, this was normal. This was how he would remain until I got him out of there.

"Hey," he said, placing his hand on the glass. On my side, I did the same. It had become a tradition since we couldn't touch each other. God, I would have given anything to climb through that stupid damn partition and hug him.

"Hey, Matty."

He stared at me for a moment, and I could feel him analyzing my expression. "Everything okay?"

I nodded. "Yeah."

He raised an eyebrow. "Okay. What's going on? You're doing that thing."

"What thing?"

"Looking at me like you're trying to pretend everything's cool when something is obviously wrong. I feel like you're about to tell me something I'm not going to like."

He took his hand away from the glass and leaned back in his chair. A little bit of the hope in his eyes seemed to flicker away, and I realized what he was thinking.

I turned around to look over my shoulder at the guard who stood by the door. He was far enough away that he wouldn't be able to hear us, but as I turned back to Matteo, I lowered my voice. "Nothing's happened, Matty. I don't have any news for you yet. This isn't over."

He nodded. "Okay. So why do you look so worried?"

"Because I…" I paused, not sure whether I even *should* have been worried. I mean, what was there to tell? The only thing that had happened was that I'd decided Drake wasn't the devil, and I'd kind of mentioned that to Matteo on the phone. So why did I feel like I was about to confess to a major sin?

"Oh God, Darcy." Matteo sighed. "This is about Drake, right?"

I hated that my cheeks began to burn because I wasn't sure I'd ever blushed in my life before. I didn't care for it. It made me feel weak. It was way too girly and mushy for me to respond that way.

"You're into him." There was not even a hint of a question in his words. He didn't need to ask, and I squeezed my eyes closed.

"Matty, I know this is messed up, but–"

"Messed up?" he hissed, leaning forward. "Darcy, barely a week ago, you were convinced he was the reason I'm in here! What the hell happened?"

"I don't know!" I hissed back. "Like I said on the phone, he's not who I thought he was. Not even close."

"Really? This *is* the same guy you believed was great at manipulation, twisting facts, and using his job to cover his own ass?"

The part of me that still held doubts squirmed, twisting my stomach into knots but, deep down, I knew my original thoughts about him were unfair. I stood by the fact that he could manipulate people if he needed to, but if he'd been manipulating me, he would never have called me out the night we met. If he was involved in this thing, he'd have let me play it my way and then taken me down when I least expected it. Instead, he'd been open. And not just open, but vulnerable.

But what if that's all part of it?

No. I'd misjudged people before, but not this time. "I was wrong, Matteo. He's a good guy."

"So, what are we talking about here?" he asked. "I mean… what is this thing with you two?"

"I can't define it right now. Neither of us wants to define anything. All we're doing is trying to get to know each other and see where it goes."

"But it's important enough that you wanted to tell me about it. So it must be more than just that."

I hated how well he knew me. My entire boyfriend history was known by Matteo, and he knew – maybe even better than I did – how into someone I was from the way I acted. Truth be told, *that* was what had scared me the most about telling him. It was bad enough that I had to admit I was into the cop I'd hated with every fiber of my being since I'd first known of his existence. But Matteo could read me better than anyone in the world, and even when I was trying to deny something to myself, he would always be there to call me out. To force me to be honest about how I felt.

Finn Drake wasn't supposed to have any effect on me. He was supposed to be an asshole. But every time I saw him, he showed me he wasn't. He got me. And that was terrifying, but for the first time in a long time, I was prepared to paddle in the dating waters and hope they didn't end up drowning me.

"Oh, Jesus." Matteo's expression softened a little. "Baby girl, you're gonna have to stop letting your emotions show on your face."

His use of his nickname for me made tears spring to my eyes. He hadn't called me that in so long. I would have clawed out anyone else's eyeballs for attempting to call me something that made me sound so helpless, but Matty was allowed to, because Matty knew me for real. Knew who I was, and never called me that in front of anyone else. Not even Rebecca.

"I only do it around you," I told him.

He shook his head. "When you really like someone, it's obvious to everyone. I haven't seen that look in your eyes for years."

"What look?"

"You look happy and scared."

I let out a small laugh. "I feel more scared than happy right now."

"I'm scared for you too because I'm in here and I can't be there to judge him for myself." He threw his head back in frustration and let out a growl. When he looked at me again, he didn't need to say anymore.

"I'm being careful, Matty. I swear."

He nodded slowly. "You always are. But… with him, can you just be extra careful? Please? I don't want to get out of here, only to end up right back in jail when I have to kill him for breaking your heart."

I chuckled. He truly was the big brother I never had. "I promise. I do believe he's genuine, but I won't rush this." *Let's just pretend I didn't have sex with him a lot last night.*

Again, Matteo closed his eyes. "Darcy, really?"

My cheeks burned hotter. "Oh my God, you need to quit reading my mind."

"Well, you need to quit smirking like you're re-living every orgasm he gave you."

I placed my head down on the table in front of me to hide my flaming face, but I couldn't help laughing at his words. If I didn't look up, we could have been back at college, sitting in a coffee shop, having this exact same conversation. As I lifted my head again, Matteo was laughing too. It was a cautious kind of laugh, one that told me he was pleased to see me living my life, but with a hint of the same concerns I held myself. Whatever those concerns, for a moment, I didn't care, because seeing my best friend's smile–a real, genuine smile–meant more than anything else in the world.

**

In the end, my visit with Matteo wasn't nearly as bad as I'd expected. I knew he wasn't thrilled with the prospect of me getting emotionally involved with Finn. He'd hated the idea of me getting close to him in any way because he was terrified I'd get in over my head. And he was right. I would have, but I still wouldn't have given up because he'd never given up on me.

I'd spoken to Finn earlier; he'd called me to assure me he was following up on some information he'd discovered, and that he'd call me back that evening to let me know more.

But he hadn't called. I wasn't sure how long I was supposed to leave it, and the wait made me anxious. But it wasn't just that. I couldn't wait to hear his voice again. Sure, he was still a little arrogant, and I wasn't sure either of us knew who the other really was yet, but he was the kind of guy I was slowly dropping my defenses for. In spite of everything, I really wanted to spend more time with him.

When my cellphone rang, I jumped so high, I swear I almost hit the ceiling. With my heart thumping, I scrabbled around to reach for it and quickly answered.

"Hey, Darcy." Finn's voice was softer than I'd ever heard it. Still with that gritty tone, but gentler. The sound caused my racing heart to calm. "So… I have some news for you."

Sitting bolt upright, I said, "What is it?"

"It's complicated. Have you eaten yet?"

I glanced at the clock and sighed. "No. I was actually trying to work up the enthusiasm to make something. Why?"

"You wanna come over to my place? I'll pick you up and we can grab a takeout or something. It'll be easier to talk face to face."

I smiled to myself. "Finn? Are you just making up excuses to see me?"

He laughed. "Me? Sweetheart, you just called me by my first name for the first time. I'm guessing you're pretty interested in seeing me too."

I left him waiting for a moment before laughing. "Okay. Sure. You don't need to pick me up, though. I can walk. It's not far."

"No," he said, quickly. "Please let me pick you up. Just give me around forty-five minutes. I've got a couple things I need to do then I'll be right there."

Forty-five minutes. That gave me enough time to change out of my work uniform, freshen up, and put on something a little more suitable for seeing Finn. Maybe fix my make-up too, and straighten my hair which was no doubt wavy and messy from being tied up in a bun all day.

"Sounds good," I told him. "I'll see you soon."

Chapter 12
Finn

I wasn't sure I liked the grin that spread across my face when Darcy agreed to have dinner with me. Finn Drake does not grin like an idiot over women. Doesn't happen. The sappy schoolboy smile had to go.

I wasn't lying when I said I needed to see her. I'd discovered some more about Rebecca, and some secrets about my own damn department that I hadn't seen coming. This whole investigation was screwed up, and I needed to let Darcy know just how high up this thing ran. There was stuff going on that even Al probably didn't know about. If he did, he'd done a damn fine job of keeping it quiet. I wasn't sure any of this was going to help Darcy get Torres out of jail, because there were people I knew, people I trusted with my life every day, who knew more than they'd ever said. Where the hell was I supposed to take this information? I barely had enough to string a conclusion together yet, but I was getting closer. And that was one of the reasons I didn't want Darcy walking to my place. Paranoid? Maybe. But I wasn't about to risk her safety. Paranoia was better than carelessness.

A knock at my door disturbed my thoughts as I pulled a clean t-shirt over my head. Straightening it up, I walked to the door and opened it to find Al standing in front of me. His appearance at my apartment threw me. This was *not* normal.

"Hey, buddy," I said. "What can I do for you?"

His shoulders were hunched, his face a little pale, and his dark hair was disheveled. Then I realized why.

Dylan stepped out from behind him, and before I could respond, the shorter, yet obviously stronger of the brothers, shoved me in the chest. I hurtled backward into my apartment, landing on my ass on the floor. Dylan's gloved fist connected with my jaw, hard enough to make my head snap to one side. The pain radiating from the side of my face left me stunned for a few seconds.

"Go, Al!" Dylan yelled. "I'll deal with Drake. Just get her here."

I heard the door slam, and Dylan grabbed me by the shirt I'd just put on and threw me across the open plan living room to the kitchen area, where I crashed into the table. This time I picked myself up faster, even though I could have sworn my jaw was broken, and my back stung from where it had just hit the table. I raised my arm to throw a punch of my own, but Dylan pulled out a gun and pointed it at my head. I stumbled back in surprise.

"Sit. Down," he said, punctuating each word carefully.

I quickly ran through my options. Sure, I could have taken him down *if* I was fast enough, but that gun was millimeters from my head, so the chances of me making it before he blew my head off were pretty slim.

Holding my hands up to show him I'd co-operate, I sat down on the chair closest to me. "Take it easy."

Dylan's eyes were cold, emotionless. *What the hell would Rebecca Torres have seen in this motherfucker?* Maybe it was the fact that he was built like a WWE wrestler–all muscle and tattoos. Dark hair just like his big brother. Sure, I get that women like that kind of shit, but he didn't have much in the way of a personality–not enough to tempt a woman from her husband for so long.

He must have been really good in the sack.

Without taking his glare off me, he whipped out a set of handcuffs from the back pocket of his jeans and snapped one around my ankle and the other around the leg of the chair. I chuckled at his lack of preparation. Did he really think one bound leg would stop me kicking his ass the second I got a chance?

"What the fuck are you laughing at?" Dylan muttered, walking around behind me.

I shut my mouth. Never a good idea to piss off a guy with a gun when you can't see what he's doing. In another second, I hissed out a breath as he grabbed my arms and swiftly bound my wrists together with some kind of cord, so tight I could feel the cuts forming already.

Yup. Now I'm screwed.

I'd been trained to deal with this kind of situation, but there's a vast difference between a hypothetical situation and the real thing. I couldn't let him see I was concerned, though. I had to keep that shit locked away because there was no way I was gonna let this fucker think I was afraid of him.

"What are you doing, man?" I asked, my voice completely calm, as if we were just having a few beers at a club. "What's this all about, huh?"

Dylan tilted his head to one side and barked out a laugh. "Please. No point pretending you don't know why I'm here. You been snooping around in things that ain't got nothing to do with you. We can't have that. Gonna have to shut you up."

"I don't know what you're talking about."

Dylan's face was inches from mine, his eyes wide and fucking crazy. "You know. Ohhhh, you know. I saw you, Drake. I saw you with that bitch friend of Torres'. You think I don't watch every move you make? And every move *she* makes? That slut's trouble and I ain't having her getting mixed up in things that don't concern her. Not now. Not now we finally got Rebecca's loser husband locked up for good."

The mention of Darcy made me flinch. Not only had I done my research, seemed Miller had too. Hadn't occurred to me he'd think about that. He wasn't exactly known for his intelligence. But Al...?

"You stay away from her," I warned. "She's not involved in anything. I met her at a bar."

"Liar!" Spit flew into my face from Dylan's snarled words. "I ain't as dumb as you think I am! Been listening in on your phone calls." He paused then a sinister smile lit up his face. "Where do you think my big brother's gone? He's gone to get your girl, and then we're all gonna have a little talk."

A little talk. Criminal speak for *we gonna kill yo' ass*.

"Please," I said, not above begging for her life. "Let her be. It's me who's been trying to figure out what happened to Rebecca Torres. Me who started uncovering shit. Darcy didn't do anything."

"And just what do you think she's gonna do when your dead body shows up in the Chicago River, huh? You think she's gonna let that go?" He shook his head, tutting. "No. We can't have her running her mouth off about what she knows."

"She doesn't know anything!" I snapped.

"She thinks I killed Rebecca! And she ain't givin' up 'til she finds some proof!"

"*Did* you kill her?" I asked, because, hell, if I was about to get shot in the face, I needed to at least know I was after the right guy before I died.

Dylan laughed again, so coldly the hairs on my arms stood on end. "You think you get to ask questions? Nope. When Al gets back here, *we* have some questions for *you*."

I was about to respond when I heard my cellphone vibrating on the table behind me. I twisted my neck around to see if I could get a glimpse of who was calling, but it was too far away. Within seconds, Dylan had snatched it up. He sneered. "Oh, look. It's Darcy."

My eyes narrowed but my heart jolted. If she was calling me, Al couldn't have got to her yet. Furiously trying to twist my wrists to loosen the binds, I said, "Gimme the phone. Now."

"Yeah. 'Cos that's why I'm here. To answer your demands." He rolled his eyes like he was bored. As I continued to struggle, he swiped the screen to answer but didn't say anything. He pressed the button to turn on speakerphone, and all I could hear was Darcy's shallow breathing.

"Hello?" she said. "Finn?"

"Darcy!" I yelled. "Lock your door! Don't answer it for anyone, and call the cops!"

I didn't care if the motherfucker shot me there and then, I just wanted her safe. Dylan launched my phone across the room and I ducked as I heard it smash against the kitchen cabinet. His eyes shifted to me, and in a cold voice he said, "You're gonna regret that."

Chapter 13
Darcy

As I came to, I was aware of two things. Firstly, my head was thumping, and secondly, something cold was touching my temple. I blinked several times, not sure I wanted to see where I was and what the hell was happening. The last thing I knew, I'd heard Finn screaming down the phone at me, and then… nothing. Lights out.

Another couple of blinks and my eyes focused on a short, muscular guy with dirty black hair who held a gun to my head and had a look of evil in his eyes.

What the hell? Where am I?

"Darcy…"

I recognized the voice as Finn's, but it was murmured, like he was in pain. Too scared to move my head, I flicked my eyes to the side, hoping I could seek him out in the living room I'd been dumped in, but I couldn't see him.

"Finn? Are you okay?" I tried to keep my voice even but there was a definite waver in it, and the gun pressed harder against my temple.

"Shut up."

I moved my eyes to the man who held my life in his hands. "Dylan Miller."

His lips turned upwards at the corners. "Very good. You're a clever girl. Not just a pretty face." With his free hand, he ran his fingers gently across my cheek, a move totally at odds with the way he pressed the gun against me. "Al. Get me something to restrain her."

Dylan grabbed at my hair, causing me to cry out in pain at the force he used to drag me across the room. As he threw me into a chair beside Finn, I finally got a chance to see why his voice had been so weak. A large purple bruise covered the lower half of his right cheek, another decorated his left eye and blood had dried on a cut on his lower lip. He was shackled to a chair by his ankle, and his hands were tied around the back of the chair. Tears filled my eyes at the sight of him and when he looked at me, fire raged in his eyes, almost knocking me off my chair with the force.

"What the fuck did you to do her, Miller!" he snapped.

Until he spoke, I'd barely registered the ache in my jaw. The confusion, the raging headache, and the gun in my face had stunned me, but it all came trickling in at once, and I let out a short, sharp cry as everything hit me.

I'd been waiting for Finn. When someone knocked on my door, I'd expected it to be him, but I was faced with Al Miller. He'd introduced himself; said Finn had asked him to collect me. Obviously, I hadn't believed that for a second, and he lulled me into a false sense of security by saying I could call Finn to check it was legit. When Finn answered the phone, he'd yelled at me to lock my doors, but it was too late. Al punched me in the face and then I woke up in what I assumed to be Finn's living room.

"Darcy, are you okay?"

Finn's voice soothed me for a second until Dylan yelled, "Fucking hurry up!"

Al rushed toward us holding handcuffs and some cord, but before he could get anywhere close to cuffing me, I raised my knee then rammed my foot hard into his stomach, forcing him backward. He was way too big for me to knock down, and as I tried to stand up, Dylan pointed the gun at me again.

"Sit."

I was torn. I wanted to get out of there alive, but I equally wanted to beat the shit out of him for what he'd done to both Matteo and Finn. The man with the gun wins every time, though, so I slowly sank back into the chair.

Al straightened up and came toward me again. Dylan stepped away so his brother could bind me to the chair, but he kept the gun trained on me the whole time. Once my ankles and wrists were bound the same way as Finn's, the room fell silent. I wanted to ask what the hell was going on, but I wasn't sure if speaking would make Dylan shoot. All I knew was that Finn and I were in a crap load of trouble and there was nothing we could do to help ourselves.

I started to shake as the realization of the situation hurtled into my brain. I'd tried. God knows I'd tried my best to help Matteo, but after just a few days, I'd screwed it all up. And now, not only was I about to die, but the only other person in the goddamn world who believed he was innocent was about to be killed too. Matteo was going to be stuck in jail for his full sentence. Most of his life would be over by the time he got out, and it was all my fault. I couldn't save him.

I'd failed.

"You know what?" Finn said, his voice a little firmer than before. "If you're gonna kill us you could at least do us the courtesy of explaining why."

"You know why," Dylan said. "Tell her what you found out, Drake. Tell her."

I turned my head toward him, remembering he had actually called me over for a reason. He'd discovered something new.

"I spent some time finding out more about Rebecca," he said, before I could ask. "You wanna know why she was blowing so many cops?"

I nodded.

"She was working undercover. My boss approached her because he knew the guys hung out where she worked, and he suspected *someone* on the team was corrupt." Finn cast a hate-filled glance at Al. "She was basically doing what you tried to do with me. Feeling some people out, finding out what kind of shit they were messing around with. Except she was getting paid for it."

"But… she would have told Matteo. And to find out information, she didn't need to be getting *that* close to so many cops. This makes no sense." I wasn't sure why I was so surprised. Nothing had made any sense over the past few days. What was one more complication in an already long line?

"I can't speak for her, but what I can tell you is that she *was* cozying up to a lot of cops to dig for information. And then this guy…" He nodded toward Dylan. "This guy got involved, and for whatever reason, she cared less about the corrupt cops and more about fucking him as often as she could."

Dylan shrugged, smirking. "I don't know what to tell ya. She couldn't get enough."

"Okay," I said slowly. "But how does this help? I mean, regardless of why she was throwing herself at all cops that came within a mile of the restaurant, that's not-"

"My boss was paying her a *lot* of money to get information," Finn interrupted. "But she was getting the kind of information he didn't want her to have." I narrowed my eyes in confusion. "Lieutenant Wood was kinda playing both sides of the fence. He wanted Rebecca to sniff out anyone in his department who was 'untrustworthy' yet he's involved in some deals that, if uncovered, would have put him behind bars for a long ass time. So, he ordered a hit on Rebecca. And knowing Al over there would do anything to keep his brother out of jail, he blackmailed Dylan into killing her to keep her quiet. It was perfect. If Dylan tried to tell anyone the truth, that he was forced into killing her, not only would nobody have believed it, but Wood would have had him arrested, if not for a crime he'd already committed, he could have framed him for something new. Once he'd set the wheels in motion, Wood knew Dylan would enlist Al's help to fit Torres up for the murder, with it being perfectly plausible that he killed her because he found out she was screwing around."

Squeezing my eyes closed, because my head was still aching and getting worse with all this new info, I said, "I… What?"

"It's amazing what you can find with a key to the boss' office and a little bit of hacking."

"But why would he kill her if he was sleeping with her?" I mumbled. Everything Finn had just said was still trying to filter into my brain, but no matter how hard I tried, I couldn't seem to make any of it sink in. "I don't understand."

"She was nothin' more than an easy lay," Dylan answered, with another shrug. Then he turned to look at me then Drake. "But here's the thing. I didn't kill her."

I wasn't sure if the blow to my head had damaged my hearing, and I glanced at Finn, as if to check. His eyes were narrowed on Dylan.

"Bullshit. If you didn't kill her, what the fuck is all this about?"

Dylan rushed Finn, crouching down in front of him and pressing the gun to Finn's forehead. "How fucking stupid are you? Huh? You found out what nobody was supposed to know. All you had to do was take it to the right person and it'd all be over for me! I didn't kill that bitch but everything was set up to make it look that way to anyone who dug around hard enough. But I didn't take that bribe so I'm already living on borrowed time here. Like you just said, Wood will find a way to make sure I pay. I didn't do what I was told. I'm just waiting for something to happen, something that will see me spending the rest of my life behind bars, and I don't need you speeding the process up!"

"And you thought killing me and Darcy would help?" Finn shook his head in astonishment. "Fuck. You're dumber than I thought. You're screwed either way."

My head was pounding more than ever as I tried to unravel what Dylan was saying. If he was telling the truth, if he didn't kill Rebecca, then who did? If Lieutenant Wood ordered Dylan to kill her and he refused, wasn't he curious about who did it? Or was he just relieved she was gone? And why the hell were we being held? Why did Dylan Miller even know about me? Again, I looked to Finn to see if he had any answers. Confusion was still heavy in his eyes and the room was silent, but the longer I watched him, the more I could see the beginnings of clarity replacing the uncertainty.

Finn looked over at Dylan. "Do you know who killed her?"

Dylan shook his head. "Not a goddamn clue."

Just like that, Finn started to laugh. Not the laugh of someone who was genuinely amused, but the laugh of someone who had just figured something out. "And you have the nerve to call me stupid. You dumb fuck."

Dylan pressed the gun harder into Finn's head. "What did you call me?"

"You heard. Lemme ask you something. Whose idea was it to bug my phone?"

"Al's. He said you thought there was something wrong with the evidence, and that if anyone was going to try and figure this out, it'd be you. He was looking out for me because he knew... oh, he knew you'd come up with something eventually, and it would come back on me. But I didn't do it!"

Finn laughed harder and Dylan's face reddened as he gripped the gun tighter, pressing it more forcefully against Finn's head. I honestly thought that, between the fear, the tension, and the headache, I was going to vomit all over the carpet. Finn's laughter was only making the situation worse but I was frozen, unable to get a word past my lips.

"The fuck are you laughing at?" Dylan yelled, lifting the gun and smashing it across Finn's face. The laughter stopped immediately, but the smirk on his face remained in place. I kinda wanted to smack him myself, but I realized that, no matter what, neither of us were getting out of there alive. Nothing was going to change that, and my chest tightened.

As Finn turned his head to look at Dylan again, I saw blood trickling down his cheek from where the gun had hit him. "You still haven't figured this out?"

"Figured what out? What are you talking about?"

Ignoring his question, Finn looked over at Al, who had been quiet the whole time. His stance was rigid, and the realization began to dawn on me too.

"Why'd you do it?" Finn asked him. "Huh? No fucking wonder you've been on my ass every minute of the day. You weren't watching out for your brother, you were watching out for yourself."

Dylan stumbled backward as if Finn's words had knocked him down. The gun dropped to the floor as he faced his brother. "What's he talking about, Al?"

Al's whole body began to shake as he straightened up to his full height, towering above us all. He didn't have the unwavering arrogance of his little brother. He was trembling, and moisture formed in his eyes.

"Al?" Dylan said again. "What's he talking about?" His voice got louder with each word.

The big bear of a man took a step forward. "It was never supposed to come to this. None of it was supposed to come to this."

"To what? What…?"

"You think you were the only one who was into her?" Al stared at his brother, his eyes wide. "You knew she was screwing around, but you had no idea just how many people she was fucking." He nodded in Dylan's direction. "Yeah. That's right. She was with me too."

My head began to spin and bile burned in my throat. I took some deep breaths, trying to stop myself throwing up. It wasn't Al's confession that shocked me; I didn't know these people. I didn't know what kind of people they were on a day to day basis, but I thought I knew Rebecca, and while I'd already learned she was nothing more than a cheating slut, finding out there was another guy to add to the list made me want to dig the bitch up so I could kill her myself. Matteo was in jail and Finn and I were going to die, all because she couldn't keep her panties on.

As Dylan's legs dropped from beneath him and he sank to the floor, Finn stared at Al. "How did you get yourself into this?"

"Same way as everyone else. She made it easy."

"You're married, Al."

"So are half the other guys who slept with her."

"Yeah, but you… fuck, I know you've done some shady stuff but I would never have put you down as a cheat or a goddamn murderer. You've been my partner for years, man.

What…? Why?"

"She was real good at her job." Al leaned back against the couch, his eyes on Finn. "She played me. Made me think I was more important than the others. She even said shit about my own brother to make me believe I mattered. She told me she'd been hired by Wood to find out if any of us guys were corrupt. Said she was only telling me because she knew I wasn't, and that she liked me the best."

I suddenly understood Finn's earlier burst of laughter. If it hadn't been so tragic, I'd have laughed too. This was manipulation 101. Jesus, for a guy in his position, of his rank, how the hell did he not see her for what she was? She'd played him all right. By telling him what she was doing and making him think he was above his boss' and her suspicion, she'd got him exactly where she wanted him. The bolder the move, the less people suspect, after all. One flutter of those overly made-up eyelashes, a pout of her perfect lips, and a flash of her boobs… for a guy like Al, that would have been enough.

A flicker of shame and hypocrisy lit inside me. Hadn't I done the same with Finn? Tried to use everything I could to get answers from him?

Big difference. You weren't doing it for your own gain, and you wouldn't have screwed the entire police department.

True as that was, it didn't sit well with me that I had anything in common with the woman I used to know as a friend.

"She said she was going to leave her prick of a husband– her words, not mine." Al glanced over at me, smirking, and my blood boiled under my skin. "She told me he was fucking useless anyway. Working a dead end job. That's why she liked me. My job matters."

"Matteo is worth a hundred of you, you lowlife sack of shit!" I spat. My whole body was twitching, desperate to get free from the binds that held me in place so I could claw his goddamn eyes out.

When he came toward me, pointing the gun in my face, I didn't care. Nothing mattered anymore. The end result was going to be the same no matter what I said to him.

"He was the one who was worthless!" Al yelled, lowering down so his eyes were level with mine. "He didn't love her the way I did! He didn't do anything in his life that amounted to anything! *She* loved *me*!"

I sneered. "She was a low-class skank who'd drop her panties for the slightest chance of making a quick buck. And you?" I looked him up and down, disgust pouring from me in waves. "If that's the kind of woman you're into, I guess you *were* made for each other. I don't know what she told you about Matteo, but if you had half a brain, you'd have had the common sense to check out her story. He's a good man. He was working two jobs to support her lying ass, while she was whoring herself out and doing God only knows what with the cash she earned. He sure as hell didn't see any of it."

Angry tears burned my eyes. It was her selfishness that had caused this. It was bad enough that she was willing to stoop so low, to get involved with a bunch of random men for money. But to know she'd been running Matteo down too? Telling lies about him? She was a special kind of evil. The only thing I could take comfort in was knowing that this showdown would end, and Matteo would never have to know just how low his so-called wife really was. He'd been hurt enough by her already.

How the hell did it ever get so far? How could she have taken the money in the first place? It was one thing to do undercover work, but why had she taken it so far? *Was* it just the money? Did she get a kick out of being wanted by so many men? Did Matteo ever mean anything to her?

Rebecca was the only one who could answer those questions, and she was gone.

"I don't believe this," Dylan said, still sitting on the floor, staring up at his brother. "All my fucking life, you've been the 'good' one. You've lectured me on how to behave, and you've tried to stop me doing stuff that would land me in jail. You've gotten me out of so many things, and you... you were just as fucking bad deep down! Worse! It's your job to keep scum like me off the streets! And you were cheating on your perfect wife and kids with my woman, and when you couldn't have her all for yourself, you fucking killed her, all the time knowing it was me that would be in the frame if you couldn't set Torres up!"

"She wasn't your woman!" Al roared, turning away from me and facing Dylan. "She was mine! I never meant to hurt her! I followed her to the club that night where she was with her idiot husband, and when she left, I followed her as she walked home, we got into a fight and..." he paused then began pacing the room. With his gun firmly in one hand, he used the other to pull at his hair. "She made me so mad. She said stuff she knew would hurt me. Said I was no use to her anymore. How could she even say that? A few days before, she told me how much she loved me, and how she wished her husband was dead so we could be together, and then she just changed her mind. I was *so* angry. I didn't think. I shot her, and then I had to fix it. Had to find a way to make sure nobody found out what I'd done or I'd lose everything."

"At my expense!" Dylan roared. "You'd have let me go down for this!"

"If it wasn't for me, you'd have been in jail years ago, you ungrateful asshole! What thanks did I get?"

"I'm here, aren't I?"

"To save your own ass! The only reason you agreed to help me shut these fuckers up was because you thought I was doing *you* a favor! It's all about you! It's always been about you!"

As Al and Dylan continued to scream at each other, I tore my eyes from them to look at Finn. Like me, he'd been transfixed on the story that had unfolded, but the second his gaze fell on me, I knew he was thinking the same as me. This was over. When the brothers finished hurling accusations at each other, they'd kill us and then each other.

His eyes were trying to reassure me that this was going to be okay, but I was looking deeper, and I could see the realization in them. My heart stilled because, like me, he wasn't scared. I didn't want my life to end, especially not like this, but I'd been cruising through each day on autopilot, my mission to help Matteo the only thing forcing me to wake up each morning. And as I continued to look at Finn, I could see that, somehow, he felt the same. I could only guess that he kept going because he loved his job, but aside from that? There was little else making him carry on.

I needed to say something to him. Something that let him know I understood. I wanted to crawl into his lap and hold onto him because, if these were going to be our last moments, I wanted to be beside someone who–for the first time in a long time–got me. Got who I was and knew that, even though I'd fought against it like crazy, I cared about him. And I knew he cared about me too.

My thoughts were cut short when the door to Finn's apartment was kicked open, and four armed cops burst in. I screamed as Al fired the gun, but with my eyes closed, I'd no idea if he'd purposely hit anyone, or if he'd just pulled the trigger from the shock of people barreling into the room. Not daring to open my eyes yet, I remained still, my whole body trembling as I prayed Finn was okay. I could hear shouting and some kind of scuffle but I couldn't make out any words.

"Darcy? Darcy, it's okay."

The chair beside me made a scratchy sound across the floor as it moved closer to me and the warmth of Finn's arm brushed against my skin. "It's okay."

I slowly opened my eyes to find him staring at me, his eyes telling me everything really was okay. Al and Dylan were both gone. Whether they were alive, I didn't know. Didn't care. But they weren't in Finn's apartment anymore.

Two cops approached us, and before I could speak, they began untying and unlocking us from the chairs. The relief when my wrists were freed was incredible, and as I brought my arms back in front of me, I rubbed each one gently, wincing at the soreness from the cuts. The second Finn was free, he sank to his knees in front of me and wrapped his arms around me, pulling me in close. My body sagged in relief and I wound my arms around him too, holding him tight as the fear rushed out of me and was replaced by warmth.

After a moment or two, an unfamiliar voice said, "You guys, okay? Do we need to get you to the hospital?"

Finn pulled back, looking a little embarrassed at his display of affection for me, and shook his head. "No. I think we're good." He glanced at me and I nodded. "We're okay."

The older-looking cop in front of us gave a short nod, patting Finn on the back.

"How the hell did you find us?" Finn asked.

The officer smiled. "You weren't the only one who thought the Millers were involved in Rebecca Torres' murder. I had a tracker on Al's phone, and on yours." He grimaced. "I'm sorry. I never thought you were involved but I knew how you felt about the verdict, and I figured if you were digging around, you might need some back up if anything happened." He shifted his gaze to me. "Once I realized you were involved with Darcy, I was fucking glad I did it." He held up his hands. "I swear I never listened in on your calls for longer than a few seconds, and I'm sorry I did this without telling you, but only a little, because things would have been real different if I hadn't."

Finn rubbed his hand across his forehead and relief crossed his bruised, battered face. "Thank you, Sampson. I thought we were dead for sure." He took a hold of my hand and looked down at me. "Are you okay?"

I nodded. "I think so. I don't know. I need a freaking drink." *The more alcoholic, the better.*

Finn and Sampson both laughed and Finn wrapped his arms around me again. "Me too."

Sampson smiled. "We're gonna need to talk to you tomorrow, but for now, you can both relax."

As he turned to leave, I said, "Wait!" He paused and turned back to me. "Thank you for what you did. But I need to know… what happens now? What will happen for Matteo?"

"We'll contact his attorney tonight if we can reach him. If not, first thing in the morning. We'll need to take statements from you and Finn and we'll be questioning the Millers as soon as we get them back to the station. When we've got everything we need, Matteo Torres will be freed."

Matteo Torres will be freed. I did it. Finn and I, in the most fucked up of ways, had done what we'd set out to do. My body collapsed against Finn's and he held me tighter. "Thank you," I said again. "Thank you so much."

Sampson winked at me. "It's all part of the job, ma'am."

As Sampson walked away, I turned to Finn as he got to his feet, glancing around at the mess that had been made. An overturned table had spilled books and paperwork all over the floor; a plant by the door had been tipped over, scattering dirt all over the cream carpet, and some of his furniture was angled wrong from being knocked as the cops had wrestled Dylan and Al out.

But then he looked at me, and it was like the mess didn't matter anymore. "Well, as dates go, this was pretty dramatic."

I held up my hands in mock horror. "Wait. This was a date?"

Finn laced his fingers through mine and pulled me in to him, wrapping my arms around his waist. "I'm afraid so. And… I think we should probably have another one. Preferably without the handcuffs."

I smirked, raising an eyebrow. "But," I murmured, pressing my lips gently to his, "where's the fun in dating a cop if we don't get to play with handcuffs?"

Desire flickered in his eyes, and his voice dropped in that husky way I was growing to love. "I knew I liked you, Darcy."

I traced my fingers gently over the bruise on his cheek, my thoughts turning serious again. Because for the past few days I'd been annoying this man who really didn't have any good reason to help me, to listen to me, or to even contemplate speaking to me again. Without him, I'd still have been facing sleepless nights, wandering around in a stressed out daze, and absolutely no further along in helping Matteo.

"Thank you, Finn. Thank you for helping me. And for taking a beating to help get Matteo out of jail. What I tried to do with you was stupid, and you could so easily have let me do things my way and… well, if Sampson hadn't been on the case too, I would have ended up dead. We both would have."

I shuddered as I thought about that possibility. And about Rebecca. The woman I'd known for so long but didn't really know at all. Although I knew Matteo would soon be free, my heart hurt for him because the truth about her would be revealed to him too, and he would be crushed. Walking out of the prison gates didn't mean instant happiness. It meant learning to accept what had happened to him, and trying to find a way to fit back into the real world again. There was a long road ahead, but I wouldn't let him do it alone. I'd be there to hold his hand the whole way.

"Hey." Finn placed a hand on my cheek, bringing my focus back to him. "I didn't expect things to go down the way they did, but I wouldn't change it." He smiled. "You might be a pushy, persistent pain in the ass, but I don't think I've ever met anyone who cares so much about other people. And… if it's okay with you, I'd like to keep you around."

"Romantic." I chuckled, then kissed him softly again. "But, you know, you're not so bad yourself, Detective Drake. And I'd like to stay."

Chapter 14
Three Weeks Later
Darcy

I stood on shaky legs outside the place that had been Matteo's home for the last year. Kept back by huge barriers and cops, the state's press had gathered, waiting to get that shot of Matteo's first moments of freedom. His release was huge news, not only because he had been falsely deemed a murderer, but because of the fact that police corruption had been highlighted by his wrongful conviction.

After that night in Finn's apartment, Al Miller had unraveled real fast. He confessed to everything, and if we hadn't all been through hell, I might have had an ounce of compassion for him. He'd been duped just like all the other guys. He wasn't a cold-blooded killer; he was a guy who'd gotten in too deep and panicked. All the same, he had murdered someone. And he'd allowed someone else to serve time for his crime. Matteo had been informed of the full truth of Rebecca's betrayal. Having to be the one to tell him had cut me in two, but after discussing it with his attorney, we agreed it would be better coming from me than anyone else. He'd been heartbroken when he found out she'd cheated, and he'd been devastated by her death. It's amazing how long a heart can continue to beat after being broken so many times, and finding out just how much of a bitch she really was had ripped him apart. The two of us had clung to each other and cried for hours the day I told him the truth. Aside from the day he was sentenced, it was the worst day of my life. The news that he was going to be released didn't soften the blow at all because that level of betrayal was beyond comprehension. It was going to take a long time for him to heal.

Matteo's parents stood beside me, and I knew Finn was just behind us, helping to control the bloodthirsty journalists. I'd wanted him with me, but he'd insisted that this moment should be family only. Matty's parents considered me one of their own, and Finn told me he didn't want to intrude. He was right to give us this time, but I still wished he was beside me, holding me up. The anticipation was making me sag under my own weight and I needed someone to keep me upright.

Alberto Torres noticed me swaying unsteadily and he wrapped his arm around my shoulders. "Easy there, Darcy. It won't be long now."

His arm provided the support and comfort I needed. He looked so much like Matteo, it was insane.

I nodded. "I know. I can't believe how long we've waited for this. I just… I wish it wasn't such a public thing."

"Me too," Adriana Torres said from her husband's other side. "This is a private moment."

Matteo's mom had been one of my favorite people since the first time I met her. She was a small, homely-looking woman with thick black hair that hung in curls around her shoulders. She'd always been so warm and welcoming to me, and Matteo had told me many times that she thought of me as a second daughter. Matteo's real sister, Lorena, was heavily pregnant and in no condition to make the journey, which made me sad, but I smiled at the thought that I'd accompany Matteo to see her soon.

The rise of chatter and the flashing of cameras alerted me to the fact that Matteo was now walking toward us. It had been forever since I'd seen him in anything other than his ugly prison clothes. He was dressed in his own jeans and one of his favorite shirts; a blue button down with a black dragon logo down the left side. He was being escorted by two prison guards and his attorney, Robert Lane, and as the gate opened and he stepped out toward us, the noise grew louder and the flashes grew brighter. I took a small step back to allow his parents the first embrace, but my heart was hammering so hard in my chest I could hardly hear anything else. I watched with tears streaming down my cheeks as my best friend was pulled into his parents' arms, all three of them crying and whispering things to each other that I couldn't hear.

From the moment I heard Matteo had been arrested for Rebecca's murder, I'd been determined to make things right. I put my faith in the cops, and in lawyers, and in a jury of strangers, and we were let down over and over. Doubts consumed me every step of the way as I tried to be the one to help him, but in my heart, I knew *this* had to be the end result. Putting my life on the line hadn't fazed me for a second because without Matteo, and without his family, my life would have been very different. Maybe I'd have been living somewhere else. Maybe I'd have been on the inside of a jail cell myself. Who the hell knew? I might not have had much, but I'd never *needed* much. Just my best friend by my side and I was set. Because having one person in my life who cared about me was more than I'd ever had growing up. Anything else was a bonus.

My breath came in short bursts as the joy of what was happening disrupted my ability to do something as basic as inhaling and exhaling. As Matteo was released from his parents, he stood perfectly still, just staring at me. His own breathing was labored as he too had tears raining down his cheeks. Then he ran at me and threw his arms around me in the fiercest hug I'd ever received. I hugged him back just as hard, squeezing my eyes closed and relishing in finally being able to hug him again. Matteo hugs were the best, and I knew that for the foreseeable future, I'd be hugging him as often as I could to make up for lost time.

He pulled back from me just a little to kiss my forehead. He opened his mouth to speak, but nothing came out, and I shook my head.

"It's okay," I told him. "I know."

"No, Darcy." He rested his hands on my shoulders. "You don't know. Nobody has ever, ever done the things you were willing to do for me. And I know I've thanked you a million times before, but I had to save this for when I finally walked out of those gates because I was so scared something would go wrong. That I wouldn't get out. You have been my best friend for so, so long, but I… I never imagined anyone would do what you did to help me. I wouldn't have expected it because none of this was your fault. It wasn't on you to get me out, but you did. And I can never repay you for that."

Shaking my head again, I said, "You already know I don't need anything from you. I just wanted you out of that hell hole."

"You almost died for me."

"Yeah. And I would do it again and again, Matty."

After staring into my eyes for another moment, he pulled me close to him again and hugged me tight. "Thank you. Thank you for everything."

"Anytime, buddy. Anytime."

As we broke apart, we both wiped away tears from our cheeks, and Adriana said, "Are you ready to face the reporters?"

"I don't have to," he said, with a small laugh. "I never asked for this attention and I don't want it."

Robert Lane stepped closer to us and smiled. "I'll be giving a statement. There's a car waiting for you right outside. All you have to do is walk by, the prison guards will get you to the car, and you're all headed for Mr. and Mrs. Torres' hotel. I've booked a private conference room for you so you guys can have a little time to catch up without being locked in a hotel room. There's food and drinks waiting for you, and I'll follow on behind you so we can talk about what happens next."

Matteo gave him a brief nod and shook his hand. "Thanks." He took a deep breath and turned to me and his parents. "You ready for this?"

"Hell yeah," I said, laughing, and his parents laughed too.

You wouldn't have thought he'd been in jail for so long. He acted like he'd just spent a few hours at work and was ready to take on the weekend. He'd been lucky in so many ways. Many other people who were innocent spent much longer behind bars. When they eventually got out, the world was a whole different place. At least for Matteo, Chicago and the rest of the world was mostly the same.

Matteo took another large lungful of air and I took his hand. On his other side, his mom did the same, and his dad stood behind us, while three armed prison guards positioned themselves around us, ready for the walk to the car. As the gate opened, we all began to walk out, and again, the intensity of the camera flashes grew stronger, and so many people were shouting for our attention that it was impossible to understand what they were saying. As we walked, I looked for Finn amongst the hordes of police officers, and when I spotted him I threw him a huge grin. I couldn't wait to see him when he was off duty, and as he winked at me, Matteo turned his head and his eyes fell on Finn. He let go of my hand and said something to one of the guards before breaking away from us and running over to where Finn stood.

My heart leapt into my throat as I watched my best friend approach my man. Finn was surrounded by police and journalists were jostling to get a shot as Matteo moved closer to them. When he reached Finn, he leaned forward and said something to Finn, and then he embraced him as if they were old friends. My tears began to fall again, because I knew it took a lot for Matteo to do that. He hadn't been certain about Finn's loyalty, even after the truth was revealed. I didn't take it personally; I knew he trusted my judgement but he'd been screwed over by cops in the worst possible way, and he was dealing with knowing his wife was a liar too. It wasn't a shock that he was suspicious of Finn, so to see him take the step to move forward from all this was as much of a gift as seeing Matteo walk free. After a couple of minutes of the guys talking, Matteo ran back over to us and I wrapped my arm around his waist, smiling up at him.

"Thank you, Matty."

He grinned. "It's the least I can do, baby girl. Finn's gonna join us in an hour or two, when's he done dealing with everything here."

I didn't think my smile could get any bigger, but I proved myself wrong. "You're the best."

"Right back at ya, Darcy."

✶✶

What followed was simultaneously one of the best and most heartbreaking afternoons of my life; and I'd been through enough bad times to make an accurate comparison. The conference room Matteo's attorney had arranged for us was incredible. Matteo's eyes almost fell out of his head when he saw the selection of food and drink laid out for us, and there were staff members on hand to get more of anything we needed. With only prison food to eat for so long, the array of sandwiches, salads, pasta and cakes seemed to blow his mind. There was enough food to feed an army, and although plenty of alcohol had been provided, we all drank sparingly because we knew there was so much to discuss.

As I sat around the table with Matteo and his parents after eating our first round of food, silence descended. It was like we were all slowly letting recent events wash over us, trying to make sense of all that had happened.

After a while, Matteo said, "You guys, I've had nothing but time to think over the last few weeks. Well, more than that, obviously. But since I found out what really happened with Rebecca, I just… I wanted to ask you… did you like her? Did you really like her? Did you ever think she would be the kind of person who would do what she did? Because I'm not sure I can trust my own judgement anymore."

He looked down at the table, his dark eyes heavy again, just as they had been when he was in prison, and both his mom and I shuffled our chairs closer to him.

"You know how I felt about her when you started dating her," I said, taking his hand. "I thought she was loud and rude and I didn't get what you saw in her. But you also know I grew to love her when I got to know her, and there was no way you could have seen this coming. I've tried to make sense of it too, because I'm not sure she was such a bitch when you met her. The only thing I can think is that she started out trying to do something good, then she got addicted to the money, and got some kind of twisted thrill out of the whole thing."

"I liked her," Alberto said from across the table. "She was real polite the first time we met her."

I laughed. "That's because Matteo had smoothed out the brashness by the time you met her."

Adriana sighed. "I didn't like her at first. She *was* polite, but there was something in her eyes I didn't trust."

Right there. She was right on the money with that. That was exactly how I felt when I saw her for the first time.

"You didn't say so," Matteo said, looking up at her.

124

Adriana shook her head. "I didn't. Because you looked so happy, and like Darcy, once I got to know her more, I loved her too. I've often thought that maybe if I'd said something back then, things would have been different but, Matteo, you wouldn't have listened. You were young and in love. All I could do was support you."

Matteo wrapped his arm around his mom. "I don't blame you, Mom. You're right. I wouldn't have listened. But I do wish I hadn't been so blinded."

Tears glistened in his eyes, and Adriana held him tighter as my heart cracked inside my chest. No matter how happy he was to be home, he was going to hurt for a long time. He'd need so much support to find a way through this.

Adriana glanced at her husband across the table, and they seemed to be having a silent conversation with their eyes. After a while, Alberto gave a nod and Adriana took a deep breath.

"Matteo, Rebecca's mom called us a couple days ago."

Matteo's head snapped up in shock. "She did?"

"Yes. She's devastated about what happened to you and mortified about the way Rebecca behaved. She wants to see you."

I had to hold in a bitter laugh because I already knew what his response would be. As expected, he let out the laugh I'd forced myself to suppress.

"Not a chance," he said, shaking his head. "I don't want anything to do with any of them after the things they said about me."

"Matteo—"

"No, Mom. I know they've lost their daughter, and I understand that all the evidence pointed to me, but they knew me. They *knew* how much I loved her, that I would never have hurt her, and they refused to listen to me when I told them I didn't kill her. They called me a liar, a murderer. I

125

think they even accused me of raping her at one point, which was insane since that word never came up once in the investigation." He shook his head again. "I don't want anything to do with them."

"Okay," Adriana said softly. "I understand. The next time she calls, I'll tell her."

"You know what I don't get?" Alberto said, reaching over for a muffin and placing it on his plate before carefully pulling it apart. "What the hell was she doing with all that money?"

"I can answer that."

We all spun around as Matteo's attorney, Robert, entered the room. He was thin as a rail, tall, balding, and dressed in a tweed suit. He looked more like a college professor than an attorney. He strode into the room with authority and took a seat beside me.

"How did everything go with the press?" Matteo asked, deflecting from the question about the money.

"Fine. I gave them the statement we wrote together, and they seemed satisfied enough. They will try to find you and they will want to talk to you. People are already contacting me about interviews on TV. I've told them you're not interested, and I will continue to do so unless you change your mind. But be prepared for people to be on your back for a while. You'll be safe here for a few nights since we booked you and your parents in under fake names. But we need to work out where you'll go after, and also find ways to support you until you get back on your feet."

Matteo took some long, deep breaths. It had to be overwhelming for him. He'd lost everything. His home, his jobs, parts of his family and most of his friends. Getting him back on his feet wouldn't be easy. I'd offered to let him crash at my place, but Robert said it was too obvious a place for him to be, and that he needed to be a little off the radar. He didn't want to switch states to live with his parents again, although we were both leaving in a couple days to stay with his family, and hopefully witness the birth of his new niece or nephew. But in the long term, he wanted to stay in Chicago.

"This brings me to the question you were asking when I came in," Robert said, sitting up straighter. "We've been through everything we could find about Rebecca, and we found a bank account she'd set up for the money she was earning on the side. Matteo, there is more than eighty thousand dollars in that account, and since you're her next of kin…"

Before any of us had a chance to react, Matteo stood up, pushing his chair away angrily and pacing the room. "You think I want that? You think I would take money she earned on her goddamn back? Fuck! I wouldn't care if she had millions; that money is dirty and if I took it, I'd be no better than her!"

My insides clenched seeing him that way. He was hurting so much and there was nothing anyone could do to stop it. He continued to pace the room, and part of me wondered if all this was too much, too fast. It wasn't like this we were having a party or anything, but he'd been confined to a small space for so long with so few people around him that it must have felt weird processing his feelings with people watching him. At least in his cell he could be angry or upset without anyone's eyes on him.

"Matteo," Robert said calmly. "I understand how you feel. But this money could help you put your life back on track. It could set you up for the rest of your life."

"I. Don't. Want. It." Matteo halted his steps and turned to Robert, eyes blazing. "I would rather live on the streets for the rest of my life than take anything from her. Donate it to charity. Give some of it to Al Miller's kids to make up for the fact that their father's a fucking scumbag. I don't care, but I don't want a cent."

Eighty thousand dollars was an amount of money neither of us had seen in our lives, and if he let it go, there was little chance he'd ever have an opportunity like this again. Yet I knew his decision was right. What if he took the money and bought a great apartment? What if he used it to set up a business? Every time he looked around at his beautiful new place, or made some cash, he'd know everything he had was because of what his wife had done to him. He'd never be able to move on from it. It would be hard enough anyway.

Matteo glanced at me. "Darcy, do you… I mean… you could use it to…"

"Nope." I cut him off. "I don't want it any more than you do."

"I know. But after everything you've been through for me…"

I shrugged. "Right now, I've never been happier. I don't need anything more than I have, Matty."

He looked over at his parents, and they both shook their heads. "No," Alberto said. "Do what you said. Donate it. If you don't want it, then give it to people who can use it for good."

Matteo turned back to Robert. "Charity it is. I'll think on where I wanna donate it."

"Okay. If you're sure."

Again, Adriana shot her gaze to Alberto, and more unspoken conversations were had. I wasn't sure if Matteo had noticed because he was still pacing, but eventually, Adriana said, "Matteo, can you come and sit down, please? There's one more thing we want to tell you."

"I don't want to sit." He ran his hands through his hair. "I need to get out of here soon."

Robert nodded. "We need to be careful, but if you want to go outside, we can make it happen."

"If you want to go on out, I'll wait in here for Finn and we'll catch up," I said. Matteo was starting to twitch, and I wasn't sure if he really needed some air or if he simply needed to be alone. My heart ached as I watched him. He was like a caged tiger, desperate for the freedom he'd only just had a taste of.

"We need to talk to you too," Adriana said, giving me a small smile. I knew she was hurting as much as I was at seeing Matteo so stressed out, so I stood up and walked over to him.

He stopped pacing when I stood in front of him, and slowly, I rested a hand on his arm. "Breathe with me," I told him, and drew in a long breath before letting it out slowly. He did as I asked, and after a minute, his whole posture relaxed. He squeezed my hand then leaned back against the wall, and I sat down again.

"What did you want to talk to us about?" I asked, because I knew Matteo still wasn't ready to talk.

Alberto smiled at me. "This is only an idea, and you can have as long as you want to think about it, so please don't feel any pressure. But, while Matteo was in prison and we had no idea what would happen, we were pulling together as much money as we could for a good lawyer. One who could do better than the one you were given at trial." He glanced at Robert. "No disrespect to you, sir, but I know how hard you guys have it. We just wanted to do the best for our son."

"I understand," Robert said. "No offence taken."

Alberto nodded then turned his attention back to Matteo and me. "The money we saved is useless to us now you're free."

"It's not useless," Matteo said. "It's yours. You should do something with it."

"We saved it for you," Adriana said. "And we want you to have it. We have all we need, but you have to start over, Matteo. It's not enough to change your lives. I wish it was. But there is enough to help you get a new place. And as a gift, we'd like for the two of you to do something you've always wanted to do. I know you've talked about going to Europe for as long as you've been friends. You've both been through so much, so we've put some cash aside to send you wherever you want to go for a few weeks."

My eyes widened and I turned to look at Matteo.

"Are you serious?" he asked, staring at his mom.

Adriana smiled. "Yes. Take your time and think about what you want to do, but the money is waiting for you. You only need to say the word."

Matteo flicked his eyes toward me and I could see the excitement building behind them. "You wanna do this?"

My own eyes probably reflected his, and I nodded. "Oh, hell yeah! But…"

With a smirk, Matteo rolled his eyes. "I know, I know. You have Finn now."

The telltale warmth in my cheeks told me I was blushing. "I do." And the thought of leaving him behind for any amount of time made my insides hurt. I was already having palpitations knowing I was leaving for a week to be with Matteo and his family. But I really wanted the trip with Matteo. Hell, he deserved it, and some time for just the two of us so we could make up for some of the time we'd missed would be amazing. "I'll talk to him about it tonight." I turned to Adriana and Alberto. "Thank you so much. This is an incredible offer."

Matteo straightened up and walked across the room to hug his parents. "Thanks, guys. I couldn't ask for better parents."

Chapter 15
Finn

I'm not a guy who gets nervous about many things. I could count on one hand the times I'd been truly afraid in my adult life. Two of those times had involved Darcy, and this one was about to involve her too.

Man, I felt sick as I was directed to the room where she was with Matteo, his parents, and his lawyer. I didn't know almost everyone in there.

When Matteo had run over to me after he was released from prison just a couple hours ago, I was a little concerned he'd lay into me. I'd done nothing wrong, but I knew from Darcy that he'd been suspicious as hell of my motives. I didn't blame him for it. And if he'd hit me, I probably would have deserved it for not trying harder for him faster than I did. Instead of greeting me with a fist to the face, he'd hugged me. Now, I ain't much of a hugger; not with guys anyway. But I was pretty damn relieved that he introduced himself that way instead of the way I'd expected. He thanked me for everything I did, and for keeping Darcy safe and not messing with her. I assured him I had no intention of hurting her, and he gave me a look that told me he trusted me. Knowing how important he was to Darcy, it meant a lot to me that he was okay with us dating.

We'd kind of made the leap from 'seeing how things play out' to 'dating' the night we almost died. That night taught me a couple of things. Firstly that it still wasn't a good idea to trust many people. Al had been my buddy for a long time, and even knowing the lengths he'd gone to to protect his brother, it didn't cross my mind for a second that he'd cheat on his family or kill anyone. The other thing that night taught me was that I still had it in me to care about someone. For the longest time, the only thing I'd cared about was being good at my job. And sure, I cared about the people who came to me and needed help, but I hadn't ever felt about anyone the way I felt about Darcy. She had my attention the second she spoke to me at Midnight Rodeo. A couple of hours with her, and I just knew she was going to be a part of my life.

Darcy Ryan was the most fearless, fierce, loyal woman I'd ever met. Beautiful, and not just on the outside. She was also the sweetest woman I'd ever known. I'd watched her heart break, not for herself, but for everything her best friend had lost. After all she'd been through, she still had so much compassion for others. She was moody as hell sometimes, and God help anyone who tried to tell her she couldn't do something, but those moments were rare, and she was worth every second.

I reached the door to the conference room and took a deep breath before knocking. It didn't feel right to just walk in.

It was Robert Lane who opened the door. He smiled when he saw it was me and not some nosy as fuck journalist trying to get a scoop. "Detective Drake. Come on in."

As I stepped inside, I said, "Please, call me Finn."

He nodded, and when he closed the door behind me, I took in the scene before me. There was a long table in the center of the room, laid out like thirty people would be eating from it instead of just five. Matteo was standing at the back of the room, as if he'd been pacing. Darcy sat beside Matteo's mom, and his dad sat opposite them. I got the feeling I'd interrupted something important, but Darcy stood up and smiled as I walked toward her. From the way she held onto me, resting her head against my chest, I knew she was exhausted, and I held her close and kissed the top of her head.

Four pairs of eyes were on us. If they weren't, I'd have kissed her lips then taken her home, but I was about to meet the Torres family instead. I still felt a little sick from the nerves. Darcy looked up at me, and although she looked drained, there was still a sparkle in her eyes. Slowly, we let go of each other but she held my hand and led me toward the people she considered her family.

"Alberto, Adriana… this is Finn Drake."

Mr. and Mrs. Torres stood up, and Mr. Torres walked around the table toward me as Mrs. Torres pulled me into a hug. "Darcy and Matteo told us what you did. I can't thank you enough."

Right away, I understood why Darcy loved them so much. Mrs. Torres was warm; the kind of mother everyone should have. As I put my arms around her, I said, "It was no problem at all, ma'am."

When she released me, she winked at Darcy, and Darcy began to laugh, her cheeks glowing.

Mr. Torres held out his hand for me to shake. "Thank you," he said. "We appreciate what you did for our son more than we can say. If there's ever anything you need, all you have to do is ask."

"Thank you, sir, but really, I'm just happy justice has finally been served and Matteo is where he belongs now."

I turned and found he was right behind me. He also reached out to shake my hand, and I smiled and accepted it. Darcy stood beside me and said, "I guess you don't need me to introduce you."

"No," Matteo said. "Drake, I know we got off on the wrong foot and–"

I held my hand up to stop him. "Please. You were right to hate me. I screwed up and I will regret that every day of my life. I should have made more noise. I should have fought harder, but–"

"Dude, really. What was going down in your department could have got you killed. It almost *did* get you killed. You did what you had to do, and you got me out. You didn't have to."

I could feel Darcy's eyes on me, and I looked down at her, wrapping my arm around her shoulders. "One look at this woman, and seeing how much she cares about you… I couldn't walk away. I couldn't walk away from either of you. I would have got you out eventually, but Darcy forced me to take a good look at myself and my team. I don't deserve any thanks. Darcy is the one who pushed this. It was all her."

The fondness in his eyes as he looked at my woman might have made another guy jealous. Maybe a few years ago, it would have made *me* jealous. But I knew I had nothing to worry about. She loved him like family. Me? Well, I wasn't sure she loved me yet, but if she did… it was definitely as more than just a friend.

Chapter 16
Darcy

Finn placed two glasses and a bottle of red wine on the coffee table, and as he sat down on the couch beside me, I smiled. It had been a long, emotionally draining day, and as much as I hadn't wanted to leave Matteo, we all needed a break. He needed some time to himself, his parents needed some rest, and me? I needed Finn.

He brought me home after we spent a couple of hours quietly celebrating Matteo's release, and then we'd both showered and changed. I was wearing my favorite oversized hoodie, and my damp hair was piled on top of my head in a messy up do. Finn had ditched his work clothes and was now wearing blue jeans and a black Chicago Bears t-shirt. Somehow, he looked even sexier when he was dressed casually than when he was wearing a suit. Although, the suit was pretty appealing too. We'd had dinner together and, with the plates all washed up, we were finally relaxing.

Once Finn had poured the wine, he handed me a glass then wrapped his arm around me. I snuggled against his chest, still completely in awe of how much difference a few weeks had made. The me who had fought against getting close to Finn had taken a serious hit the night we'd almost got killed, and seeing how hard he worked to get Matteo released quickly had weakened me more. But that day, watching him make such an effort with Matteo and his family… I was done. I had no fight left in me. It was time to give in.

Of course, there was still one thing I needed to talk to him about. The European trip. I hadn't had much time to even discuss it with Matteo beyond us agreeing we wanted to go. We wouldn't go right away because of practicalities. Matteo needed to get a new place and a mountain of other things, and I had to arrange time off work. The issue was, if we left it too long, would I want to leave Finn at all?

"What's on your mind, baby?" Finn asked, his fingers gently playing with my hair.

My head was buried so far into his chest, he couldn't even see my face. What the hell was I giving away with my body language that he always knew what I was thinking?

"I'm gonna need you to stop reading my mind," I said, laughing softly.

"You're an open book, sweetheart." His words were laced with humor and I chuckled again.

"Only for you." I lifted my head for a second and he kissed me before I snuggled into him again. God, I loved it there. I loved his warmth, his strength. He smelled like my shower gel because he hadn't brought his own, but that didn't matter; there was no other place I wanted to be right then.

"So…?"

"Do you remember me telling you Matteo and I had a deal that one day we were going to travel together?"

"Sure."

"Well, it was always just something we talked about. A dream we knew we'd never achieve because we both failed at nailing a good job in spite of our awesome college degrees."

Finn laughed. "I'm sure you told me you'd both decided you weren't ready for grown-up jobs yet."

"Also true." Matteo and I were still young enough that we wanted to enjoy ourselves. Even though he'd got married and had responsibilities, he and Rebecca still liked to have a good time. We all had plans to grow up in a year or two, but we'd also wanted to make the most of our youth while we could. Maybe if this trip went ahead, I'd spend some time thinking about what my next step would be when it came to my career. I couldn't stay at the coffee house forever. Well, I could, but that would have been a waste of my education. I had to at least try. I shook my head to clear my thoughts so I could continue. "So… Matteo's parents were saving some money to get him a good lawyer. Now he doesn't need one, so they've offered to pay for that trip we always wanted to go on."

I felt his body stiffen slightly beneath me, and I sat up so I could look at him. He didn't look mad or upset, just thoughtful.

"You wanna go?" he asked.

I nodded. "I really do. I've never traveled before and it might be my only chance to do something this big and crazy."

"You don't wanna travel with me?" He raised an eyebrow and I smiled.

"I would love that." I pressed my lips to his. "There are so many places to go, Finn. But this trip… it would actually be a dream come true. And that doesn't happen too often."

Finn's arm tightened around me. "Are you asking for my permission, Darcy?"

"Kinda. I guess." I squirmed a little. I'd never asked anyone for permission for anything in my life.

He smiled and shook his head. "You don't need my permission. If you want to go, you should go."

I sat up straighter. "Seriously?"

"Seriously. Darcy, we've been together thirty seconds. Matteo is your family. If you wanna go places with him, I'm not gonna stop you." He placed his hand on my cheek. "That doesn't mean I won't miss you. I'm already hating that you're leaving in a few days. But I know who you are. I trust you."

It was in that exact moment that I knew for sure I felt the same. I trusted him the way I trusted Matteo. And that was huge. It had taken Matteo years to fully earn my trust, but

Finn? This was different. I was older, I understood more, and I knew I was safe with him.

I smiled up at him. "Thank you."

"Besides…" Finn placed his glass on the table then took mine and rested it beside his. He pulled me onto his lap and circled his arms around me. "…I'm not crazy enough to think I could control you. From the night I met you, I knew. You ain't a woman who does as she's told. And I never want to change that."

I laughed softly. "I don't know about that. There are some times when I'm more than happy to be controlled."

"Oh, I know." Finn shuffled slightly and I chuckled at the effect the conversation was having on him. There was a sudden prodding sensation near the top of my leg, and I shifted my position, turning around so I could wrap my legs around him, straddling him. His blue eyes sparkled when he smiled at me. "And here I was thinking you'd be too tired tonight."

He must have been crazy. I couldn't imagine ever being too tired to spend the night making love to him.

Making love? Who are you, Darcy Ryan?

My whole body seized up as those words danced around my brain. The me I used to be, the me I used to know, would have thought, *'I couldn't ever imagine being too tired to spend the night bouncing up and down on his dick.'*

Holy. Crap.

I'd never been in love before. Never even been close, really. And the one time I thought I might have been didn't feel anything like this. I always thought of love–romantic love–as being something that was achievable for others, but not really for me. It meant being vulnerable, allowing someone to see you at your absolute worst. Letting someone know things about you that nobody else knew, and that shit just didn't work for me. To me, all those things meant fear.

Constantly waiting for that person to let me down, and then having to deal with the fallout because I'd allowed myself to get too close.

Finn had already seen me at my worst. He'd seen me when I was desperate and scared and angry and bitchy. He'd seen past it all. He'd found my ice-covered heart and plucked it from my chest, replacing it with his until they'd both thawed.

My whole heart belonged to him.

"What's wrong?" Finn asked, and I blinked the fog away from my eyes and looked into his.

I couldn't help myself; I started to laugh.

How had it been this easy?

I wrapped my arms around his neck and pressed my mouth against his. "Nothing's wrong." Smiling as I looked into his eyes, I said, "I love you, Finn."

His lips curled upwards and his eyes sparkled more than I'd ever seen them sparkle before. "Oh yeah?"

"Yeah." I threw my head back, laughing. "I, Darcy Ryan, am in love with you."

Finn slipped his hand into my hair and kissed me. "I love you too, Darcy."

And there it was. The moment everything fell into place.

The doubts I'd had about Finn before I knew him were more than reasonable, but now? Now I knew better. I knew who he was, and I knew what we would have.

The doubts were gone.

About The Author

Kyra Lennon is a self-confessed book-a-holic, and has been since she first learned to read. When she's not reading, you'll usually find her hanging out in coffee shops with her trusty laptop and/or her friends, or girling it up at the nearest shopping mall.

Kyra grew up on the South Coast of England and refuses to move away from the seaside which provides massive inspiration for her novels. She published her first novel in July 2012, and her novella, *If I Let You Go* and *Blindsided (Game On Book 2)* soon followed.

To find out more about Kyra, check out her website, follow her on Twitter, Facebook or Pinterest, or drop her an email at kyralennon@gmail.com.

Other Books by Kyra Lennon

<u>The Game On Series</u>
Game On
Blindsided
A Very Game On Christmas (super short novella, not a complete story)
Sidelined
Play On
Final Score Part One
Final Score Part Two

<u>The Razes Hell Series</u>
Nobody Knows

<u>Novellas</u>
If I Let You Go
And It All Comes Down To You

Made in the USA
Columbia, SC
24 November 2017